S0-EHZ-961

FIGHT TO THE DEATH

Coburn roared in hatred and opened fire with the smoking gun clenched in his massive fist.

Ki felt the burn of a bullet striking his shoulder. He felt himself spin halfway around, and then Coburn cursed and fired again. The samurai dropped and rolled, knowing he was going to die unless he could find cover. But the giant pounced on him, grabbed his hair, and tried to break Ki's neck. Ki twisted onto his back and kicked the giant in the belly. Coburn grunted but did not move.

"I'm going to break you in half with my own hands," Coburn shouted.

*   *   *

SPECIAL PREVIEW!

**Turn to the back of this book for a special excerpt
from an exciting new western series . . .**

Gunpoint

*. . . the shattering story of a deadly blood feud by America's
new star of the classic western, Giles Tippette.*

THE BOOKTIQUE
711 Penn St.
Hollidaysburg, PA 16648

DON'T MISS THESE
ALL-ACTION WESTERN SERIES
FROM THE BERKLEY PUBLISHING GROUP

THE GUNSMITH by J. R. Roberts
> Clint Adams was a legend among lawmen, outlaws, and ladies. They called him . . . the Gunsmith.

LONGARM by Tabor Evans
> The popular long-running series about U.S. Deputy Marshal Long—his life, his loves, his fight for justice.

LONE STAR by Wesley Ellis
> The blazing adventures of Jessica Starbuck and the martial arts master Ki. Over eight million copies in print.

SLOCUM by Jake Logan
> Today's longest-running action western. John Slocum rides a deadly trail of hot blood and cold steel.

→•← **WESLEY ELLIS** →•←

LONE STAR

AND THE BUCCANEERS

J

JOVE BOOKS, NEW YORK

LONE STAR AND THE BUCCANEERS

A Jove Book / published by arrangement with
the author

PRINTING HISTORY
Jove edition / October 1992

All rights reserved.
Copyright © 1992 by Jove Publications, Inc.
Gunpoint excerpt copyright © 1992 by Giles Tippette.
This book may not be reproduced in whole or in part,
by mimeograph or any other means, without permission.
For information address: The Berkley Publishing Group,
200 Madison Avenue, New York, New York 10016.

ISBN: 0-515-10956-8

Jove Books are published by The Berkley Publishing Group,
200 Madison Avenue, New York, New York 10016.
The name "JOVE" and the "J" logo
are trademarks belonging to Jove Publications, Inc.

PRINTED IN THE UNITED STATES OF AMERICA

10 9 8 7 6 5 4 3 2 1

Chapter 1

Jessica Starbuck was weary. For three weeks she and her Circle Star crew had been rounding up cattle in the far reaches of her huge Texas ranch. It had not been an easy job. The range was dry and the weather was hot. The Texas longhorns, ornery under the best of circumstances, had been particularly mean spirited during this roundup. But even so, Jessie, her samurai friend Ki, Ed Wright, her foreman, and her cowboys had been successful in rounding up enough cattle to ship down to Corpus Christi on the Gulf Coast.

Jessie brushed back damp tendrils of her strawberry blond hair and surveyed the cattle, horses, and men. It had been a difficult time, but soon they would be able to leave. Her contract called for delivery of the cattle to her old friend James Stanford, a trader and successful businessman in New Orleans. Mr. Stanford had been a big help over the years, and Jessie was eager to deliver this herd on time. She knew that if she was successful in delivering these cattle, it would be not only a help to her, but also very important to Mr. Stanford.

1

There was another reason for shipping the cattle. The weather had been very dry and southern Texas had been gripped by drought, and with this terrible heat, Jessie knew that her few precious earthen dams and reservoirs would soon be drying up. Therefore, it was important that she reduce the size of her herds as much as possible before the really hard, hot months of the summer.

Jessie smiled wearily when she saw her foreman come galloping up. "What do you think, Miss Starbuck?"

"I think it's going to be all right," Jessie said. "The cattle are thin but there is still enough graze that we can move them on down to the coast, and perhaps fatten them up where the grass will be a little better down around Corpus Christi."

"There may be trouble," Ed said. "I've heard that there are rustlers down that way and several herds have actually disappeared."

"I heard the same thing," she said, looking troubled, "but we will take enough men to protect the herd. I would like you to stay at the Circle Star, Ed."

He blinked in surprise. "Stay? But why?"

"I need you here," Jessie said. "We still have four or five thousand head of cattle on the northern range, and we know that they are going to have to be moved around frequently in order to have enough feed and water. Also we've had some trouble with cattle rustlers. I have to leave you and most of the crew here to protect the main part of the herd."

Ed Wright was not pleased. "Miss Starbuck," he said, his voice faintly pleading, "it's dangerous for you to take just a handful of men and drive a thousand head of cattle all the way down to Corpus Christi."

"I know," Jessie said, "but I'll have Ki with me and we'll take enough men so that with a little luck we can be there inside of two weeks."

2

"I think it's a mistake," Ed said. "I really wish you would reconsider."

Jessie was about to say something, but just at that moment a particularly large brindle longhorn steer shot out of the gathered herd and headed for the high chaparral. Ed reined his horse around so that it spun on its back legs, and horse and man took off after the steer, along with several other cowboys. Jessie watched with satisfaction as she saw her foreman, not a young man anymore, begin to twirl his lariat overhead. His horse, a strong sorrel, quickly overtook the racing steer. Ed threw his loop cleanly and it landed over the horns. He flipped the rope slack over the rump of the steer, then took off at an angle, cutting the back legs out from under the steer. The huge animal did a complete somersault, and when it landed, Jessie heard the air gush from its lungs.

For a moment the steer lay stunned. Ed drew his horse to a sliding stop and turned around. While the steer was still dazed, he dismounted, removed his lariat, and remounted as he coiled his rope.

Jessie heard her foreman say, "I don't think we'll have any more trouble from this one, boys."

The cowboys nodded with satisfaction and Jessie was pleased. Ed Wright was the kind of a foreman who set an example for his men. He had spent his whole life working with cattle, and Jessie considered herself extremely fortunate to have a man of such high caliber. Ed could easily have had his own ranch and herd, but because he had been a friend of Jessie's late father, Alex Starbuck, and because of his great loyalty, he had stayed with the Circle Star for many years.

Jessie knew that the success of her ranch had been very much dependent upon the help of her foreman and a loyal crew composed not only of Texas cowboys, but also skilled vaqueros. She felt a real sense of loyalty as she watched her men expertly move the herd down toward the ranch, where the cattle would be held until they were ready to leave. Her crew worked like a well-oiled machine. There was very little wasted motion. There were few orders given. Every man seemed to know exactly what to do.

Jessie loved these roundups, and had the circumstances been a little more pleasant, she would have enjoyed this one very much. Unfortunately, there was a sense of urgency about this drive, not only because of her responsibility and her sense of duty to her old friend, James Stanford, but also because Ed had been correct in stating that there had been serious attacks on cattle drives.

Also, she had never seen the Circle Star Ranch look so stark and dry. Reservoirs that for years had been full now lay mud-cracked, hot, and sun-blasted. There was still a long, hot summer ahead of them, and Jessie knew that men, horses, and cattle would all suffer. Driving this thousand head of cattle to Corpus Christi would, however, ease some of the difficulty and, with a little luck, might possibly save the rest of the herd.

All the rest of that afternoon Jessie worked helping her cowboys move the bawling, weary herd on down toward the huge corrals near the Circle Star Ranch headquarters. As evening set over the dry, dusty land, the huge orange ball of the sun blistered and turned red. It brought no coolness, however, only the faint first stars, as it slid into the western horizon.

Jessie was weary—bone weary. She had been on this roundup for too long, and since it was her custom to live and work right alongside her cowboys, she knew that she must be a fright. Her strawberry blond hair was tangled, her men's Western shirt was crusted with sweat, her tight-fitting Levi's were dirty, and she longed for nothing more than a

4

cool glass of water and a warm bath.

But it had been good work, and she was satisfied. Now, as they approached the Circle Star's headquarters, she could see the silhouette of the ranch house, bunkhouses, cookshack, and all the other outbuildings that comprised her ranch. When Jessie saw it, she felt an immense sense of pride. It had been her father who had had the dream of the Circle Star Ranch.

Alex Starbuck had begun his march toward prosperity and fame when, many years earlier, he opened a small import-export business on San Francisco's Barbary Coast. He proved to be an extraordinarily good businessman, and soon his export business began to prosper beyond all expectations. He took several trips into the Far East, where he learned the language and cultures of those people. Within a few years he had bought sailing ships. First he bought wooden hull ones; then later, being boldly innovative, he had their hulls lined with steel. Finally he began to branch out into other enterprises.

Within six years of beginning his small one-man business, he had built an export and import business empire, employing buyers in Asia and the Far East, and developing his own shipyards. But even that had not been enough. As his fortune multiplied, Alex Starbuck bought rubber plantations in South America, steel mills in America and in other parts of the world, railroads, and other ranches. By the time Jessie's father was in his late forties, he was recognized as being one of the wealthiest and most influential businessmen in the world.

Jessie sighed. That had been his downfall, really. Against him had formed an evil cartel of powerful international figures who were bent on capturing the world's money market and grasping a stranglehold on the world banking system. Being one of the wealthiest men in the world, Alex

Starbuck, of course, figured prominently in their plans. But when he angrily refused to have anything to do with the cartel, they turned their vengeance upon him and he was murdered.

Seeing the ranch now, remembering the great pride her father had taken in buying the land, overseeing the construction, stocking the ranges with cattle, hiring the men, taking a real part and setting his roots deep down into the Texas soil, Jessie felt a great sense of sadness. In the intervening years since her father's death she had tried to carry on the tradition of her family. She had expanded the ranch, overseen the far-flung empire that her father had kept, and actually increased its profits with shrewd management and her ability to hire excellent people worldwide.

Jessie still spent a good deal of her time with international correspondence as she oversaw her father's empire. But it was here at the Circle Star Ranch where she felt true peace. Always it was here in Texas with the cattle, the men, the sweat, the dust, and the horses where she was happiest.

As they drew nearer the ranch and the longhorns moved toward the huge corrals, Jessie saw a lone figure come galloping forward out of the dust. She knew it was Ki, her samurai friend and loyal protector. Ki had once been her father's protector, too, and had saved Alex's life on many occasions. Now he had assumed responsibility for Jessie's safety.

The samurai was an extraordinary man and just seeing him made Jessie feel safe and protected. He was not only her guardian, but also her friend. And even though his customs were oriental and his dress highly unusual in the West, the few who knew Ki held him in the highest regard.

"Here he comes," Ed Wright said wearily. "I'm sure he wasn't pleased to stay at the ranch during this roundup."

6

"No," Jessie conceded. "He wanted to come along, but you know Ki. He's extraordinarily good with weapons but he is not a cowboy and he simply gets frustrated trying to throw a rope."

Ed Wright nodded. "Anyone would get frustrated. These cowboys have spent most of their lives moving cattle, learning how to use a lariat. Our vaqueros are the finest horsemen and ropers on the face of the earth. The trouble with Ki is he wants to be perfect in everything."

Jessie laughed. "Of course, and he almost is, except when it comes to cowboying."

Ed chuckled. "Why don't you go ahead and me and the boys will move the cattle on into the corrals. When do you want to start your trail drive to the Gulf?"

Jessie pushed back her Stetson. "We're going to have to leave soon, Ed. I was thinking a week originally, but now I'm thinking perhaps we should leave in just a few days. These cattle need to be grained and we have grain in the barns. They also need to be well rested and we need to prepare wagons with lots of water barrels and feed for the horses and men. It's going to take us a few days."

"Few days!" Ed Wright said. "It'll take at least a week. I still think we ought to hold—"

Jessie interrupted him. "No, Ed. I need a few extra days of safety margin. I figure if we leave a little early, that'll just give us a little more margin. I have to have those cattle in Corpus Christi by July seventh. That's when I've signed the contracts for loading our cattle."

Ed frowned. "But the ships will wait. They always do. Nobody's on time."

"We will be," Jessie said flatly. "When I give my word to do something, then you know it's important to me to do it just exactly as I've promised. Besides, James Stanford does need those cattle on a certain date in New Orleans, and if there is bad weather in the Gulf, then it might take a few extra days."

"I understand. How is Mr. Stanford doing?"

"I'm not sure," Jessie said. "I've heard he's had a few financial setbacks and his health is not what it used to be. I understand his wife is also very ill, and he has spent a lot of money taking her to New York and getting eastern doctors to help her. That's why I think, though Mr. Stanford hasn't come right out and said it, this deal is very, very important to him. Since he was such a wonderful friend of my father, it is also important to me."

Her foreman understood. He had been with Jessie enough years that he realized her great sense of loyalty. That was one of the things he had most appreciated in her father, Alex. Alex had been the kind of a man who, though incredibly wealthy, had made his deals on the shake of a hand. His word had been his bond, and so it was with his daughter.

"Don't worry," Ed promised. "We will have this herd ready to leave in two, maybe three, days. You will be taking the samurai, won't you?"

"Of course."

"Good. Well, I guess I'd better be moving these cattle along. The boys are getting mighty weary."

"There'll be plenty of food," Jessie said. "As soon as they arrive I'll make sure our cooks make something special for dessert. Also, there will be a little whiskey for after dinner."

Ed grinned. "The boys will appreciate that."

Jessie said, "You know I don't approve of whiskey drinking on the ranch, but after the rough time we've had with rounding up this herd, I think it's in order. Besides, it's going to be a long, hard drive to the Gulf. See you later, Ed."

8

Jessie touched spurs to her palomino horse, Sun, and the magnificent animal galloped forward. Within a few minutes, Jessie joined Ki.

"You look tired," the samurai said. "Bone tired."

"Thanks," Jessie said with a weary smile. "You, however, look very rested."

Ki realized his mistake. "I didn't mean that you look bad. You never look bad. You are always beautiful. But sometimes, it seems to me, you do work a little too hard."

"Phooey," Jessie said. "I enjoy the roundups as much as anyone. I would never be the kind of an owner who would simply manage from a distance. Even though Ed is totally capable of taking care of everything, I feel a sense of responsibility and I do love working with cattle and horses."

Ki nodded his head in understanding and said, "Cattle are very stupid, and the horses are not much better."

Jessie laughed. "You only say that because cattle don't respond as you would wish and horses . . . well, you would rather run than ride a horse."

Ki chuckled softly. "A man should not rely entirely on animals for transportation. He should keep himself fit, always be able to take care of himself with nothing but his own will and strength. I run because it keeps me in good condition."

Jessie understood this. Ki was a marvel of fitness and very proud of his conditioning. "Come on," she said, "let's gallop on into the ranch. I can hardly wait for a bath and feather bed."

That evening Ki, Jessie, and Ed sat on the porch, hearing the bawling of the herd in the corrals. Jessie looked up just in time to see a shooting star.

"That's good luck," she said to the two men.

"Is that so?" Ed asked.

"That's right," Jessie said. "My father always told me seeing a shooting star was good luck."

"You'll need luck," Ed replied. "It's a long ride and there are many dangers that—"

Jessie interrupted. "Now let's not go into that, Ed. We've already been over that, and I'm sure that we'll do just fine."

The Texas ranch foreman sipped his whiskey with a worried expression on his lean, weathered face. "I hope so," he said, "but I sure wish that I was going along and you were taking a few more of the boys."

"We've been through that before," Jessie said. "Stop worrying! You and Ki together could worry down a mountain."

Ed chuckled. "Jessie, somebody's *got* to worry because you never do."

Jessie said nothing. It wasn't true, of course. She was plenty worried about this cattle drive down to Corpus Christi, and she was worried about the drought and the condition of the cattle and the men. But, with luck, and a little savvy, they would do just fine. Once she got to Corpus Christi, she would buy presents for her men and give them all a bonus for work well done.

"I'm going to bed," she said, rising from her chair. "The next few days are going to be even harder than those that have just passed. I want to leave in three days, Ed."

"Three days, huh?" he said. "Well, okay, we'll just do it."

"Thanks," Jessie said as she turned and went back into the house.

★

Chapter 2

The sun was coming up, and although it still had not left the curve of the earth, the day was already very warm. Jessie could see dust hanging in the air over her herd, and her cowboys and vaqueros rode nervously back and forth, anxious to leave.

Ed and Ki rode at her sides, and Jessie now turned to her foreman. "This is it, then. We're leaving. Good luck!" She extended her hand, and it was engulfed by Ed's huge rough paw.

"Dammit, Miss Starbuck," he said, "I sure do—"

"I know," Jessie interrupted. "You wish you were coming along and you wish I were taking more cowboys. But you need to stop worrying. You've got more than enough to do. With any luck at all, we'll be back inside six weeks. You are going to have a difficult time here of your own, Ed, just keeping the main herd in graze and water."

"We'll do fine," Ed told her. "Don't fret about us. It's you that faces the most danger. Ki, you take good care of her, now."

The samurai nodded. "I will."

11

"Let's go!" Jessie said, squinting back at the sun. "There's no sense waiting any longer."

She removed her Stetson and made a circling motion overhead, the signal that they were to leave. There was no whooping and no excitement from the cowboys as they opened the gates and their herd began to crowd outside. Almost immediately the men pressed in closer, driving the cattle southeast toward Corpus Christi. Jessie did not look back at Ed or her ranch house. Instead she set her eyes straight forward and led her herd the way her father would have had he still been alive.

That first day they covered twenty hard miles, and by the end of it the cattle were bawling, distressed by the lack of water and feed. From past trail drives Jessie knew where there was a small creek that sprang from some low sunblasted hills. The creek fed into a great pond, which seeped out into the prairie, creating several acres of grass. This grass was a godsend, and after drinking their fill, the horses and cattle began to feed with contentment.

"They'll be okay now," Jessie said. "Once they've got their bellies full they'll bed down well for the night. Tomorrow if we make as many miles, we'll find another small creek where we can make camp."

Ki nodded. "Then every night there will be water and grass?"

That was a question Jessie could not answer. "I can't say. In good years, there is always water and grass in this part of the country. More and more, in fact, as we get closer to the Gulf. But in a year like this, while in a drought, well . . . we'll just have to see. One day at a time. That's how we'll take it."

Ki nodded. After sundown, when they had eaten and Jessie had posted sentries for the night, he moved off into the darkness, taking his blanket and his weapons. The samurai preferred to sleep alone at night in order to hear any sounds of approaching danger. He was Circle Star's outpost—its

12

first guard against Indians or cattle rustlers. Jessie knew that with Ki, perhaps a mile out in the hills by himself, no one would be able to approach without being seen and heard. The samurai slept lightly. This cattle drive would not be caught by surprise.

Jessie went to bed that night bone weary, but satisfied that the first day of the trail drive had gone well. If they could maintain this pace, they would find grass and water. If there were no cattle rustlers and no Indians to attack them, they would reach Corpus Christi well before July 7. The odds were, however, that there would be trouble.

In the morning, when Jessie woke before dawn, coffee was already brewed and their chuck wagon cook had steaks and potatoes frying.

"Good morning, Miss Starbuck!"

"Good morning, Hank," Jessie replied, grinning at the famed ex–bronc buster with his lined face. "I hope you cooked plenty. The men are hungry."

"Always," Hank said. "I always cook plenty of food, you know that."

"Of course, you do," Jessie said. "And you know that I spare no amount of money in making sure that my crews are well fed."

"You sure do, Miss Jessie. I don't know another rancher who feeds as good."

"Thanks," Jessie said, taking her plate, laden with steak and potatoes, and a cup of coffee and moving off. She squatted down in the prairie and ate silently, as did the cowboys. By the time the sun was up, they were again on horseback, moving the herd. The cattle, having drunk their fill, were easy to drive. Already they were beginning to understand the mechanics of the trail drive, and there were fewer and fewer steers or cows that tried to escape into the brush. Jessie knew that within three or four more days the entire herd,

13

unless stampeded by unknown forces, would continue almost placidly on down to Corpus Christi.

For the next three days the cattle drive went without incident. Each day they covered between twenty and thirty miles, depending on the terrain, and there was no trouble at all. However, on the fourth day, Jessie looked to the east and saw a huge dust storm moving toward them. They were exposed on a low plateau affording very little coverage. Jessie was immediately concerned, as were the cowboys.

"There's a canyon just up ahead," she said.

One of the cowboys, an older man named Deke Jones, who had been with her for many years, shouted, "Miss Starbuck, we better get these cattle movin' right away, or that storm is going to overtake us before we can reach that canyon!"

"Then, let's head 'em out!" Jessie shouted, as she pulled off her Stetson and waved it in the air.

The cowboys did not need to be told. Almost immediately they pushed the herd into a fast trot toward the canyon. Each one of them kept looking over his shoulder, watching as the dust storm grew larger and darker. They could feel the air change. It suddenly grew very still and they heard a growing roar. This was more than a dust storm, Jessie realized. It was a full-fledged Texas tornado!

"Make 'em run!" Jessie cried.

The cowboys drew their six-guns and began to fire. Suddenly the air was full of the sound of galloping hooves and bawling cattle. The steadily growing roar of the tornado followed them as they raced toward the canyon. Jessie hung back despite several cowboys yelling at her to move to the front. She hung back because she would not have felt right running for her own safety ahead of the herd.

When they were yet one half mile from the canyon, the tornado struck them with a fury. The air was suddenly filled with dust, flying tumbleweeds, brush, and debris.

14

Jessie choked and could hardly breathe. The cattle, which had moments before been racing ahead of her, suddenly disappeared. The wind shrieked like a banshee, and her horse staggered as the outer force of the tornado struck.

Jessie's greatest fear was that Sun would fall or even be sucked up in the tornado. Spurring hard, she raced blindly ahead, knowing that the canyon could not be very far. The tornado seemed to last for hours, and yet it was just minutes until it suddenly began to diminish and visibility cleared. Jessie looked up and realized that they were within the huge rock-wall confines of the canyon. The herd had funneled through the narrow box canyon, turned, and was now trying to stampede back out into the tornado. But Jessie and the cowboys were able to hold it.

The tornado soon passed, and then the earth and the sky seemed very still and very clear. They watched from the entrance of the canyon as the dark cloud of the tornado snaked its way south.

"We were lucky," Ki said. "Very lucky!"

"Not all of us were lucky," Deke said.

Jessie looked around, saying, "What do you mean?"

"We lost Johnny."

Jessie followed Deke's eyes to where, up near the head of the canyon, Johnny lay beside his horse. The horse and man had been cruelly trampled by the herd. In the dust and the confusion, Johnny's horse must have lost its footing and fallen.

Jessie's mouth pinched down at the corners and tears filled her green eyes. "He was a mighty good man."

"He was good," Deke said, "and he was gonna get better. Johnny was only seventeen years old, you know."

"Did he have any relatives?"

"I don't think so," Deke said. "He never spoke of any family. Best I could tell is he came from the South wantin' to be a cowboy, somewhere in Virginia, I think."

"If he had a family," Jessie said, "I'll find them, no matter how difficult that might be."

"I don't think he had one," Deke said again. "He never spoke of no family. Said he was an orphan. Johnny said his mom died when he was young, and he never spoke about his father, sisters or brothers. He just wanted to be a top hand on the best outfit in Texas. Miss Starbuck, there's nothin' you can do—nothin' any of us can do—to change what happened."

"I know," Jessie said, riding her horse over next to the still body and dismounting beside the other cowboys. "We'll bury him deep and cover his grave with rocks so that the animals can't get at it. I've got a Bible in my saddlebags, and we'll say a few words. Then we have to move on."

The other cowboys nodded, and within an hour a grave had been scraped out of the hard, rocky ground, and young Johnny had been laid to rest. Heavy rocks were placed over the grave so the coyotes and other animals could not desecrate it, and Jessie spoke a few words from her Bible.

She read the Lord's Prayer, and spoke about how Johnny had been a good cowboy. "When he came here," she said, "he didn't know anything, but I could see that he was determined to learn. He always tried. He wasn't blessed with the most talent. He wasn't our best roper or rider. He made mistakes, as we all make mistakes, but I always knew that I could count on him to do what he was supposed to do. He became a top hand—just as he set out to. We all respected his grit and determination and we'll all miss him."

The cowboys nodded solemnly. "May he rest in peace," Jessie said. "May the Lord receive him, and may he have a good horse in heaven."

With that said, Jessie closed the Bible and everyone remounted. The Texas longhorns had begun to calm down from the terror of the tornado, and now Jessie and the cowboys spoke softly and rode slowly among them. The cattle moved in a line out of the box canyon and continued on to the south.

Ki, who had remained silent and usually had very little to say unless it was important, rode beside Jessie. "Now," he commented, "Johnny's death was just a freak accident, Jessie. I know you feel guilty about it, but you shouldn't. It was just something that could not be anticipated."

"I know that," Jessie said. "Tornadoes come and go but you never really expect one is going to actually strike your herd. It was as if the tornado was bent on destroying all of us."

"No," Ki said, "it was not that way at all. It was just an unpredictable act of nature."

Jessie nodded her head. Ki was right, but she was superstitious enough to think that sometimes when things began to go bad, they would continue to get worse.

"I'll be glad when this trail drive is over," she said. "I really will be glad."

Ki felt the same way. His main concern was Jessie, not the herd. But having also listened to stories about cattle rustlers on this trail to the coast, he was more than a little concerned.

"I think," Ki said, "as we go deeper south we should double the guard at night."

"Good idea," Jessie said, as she rode on, thinking about Johnny and wondering if perhaps he did have some family in the South. Johnny was an enigma. He had no past, really. His life had begun when he became a cowboy, which is all he ever wanted to become.

Jessie had spoken with the young cowboy many times. Johnny knew he was not going to get rich or become a famous rancher. But Johnny had always tried as hard as he could, and now, suddenly, he was dead. It was a tragedy. Jessie felt a deep sense of sadness about it but struggled to expel the tragedy from her mind as the herd moved along.

That evening, they discovered that the spring Jessie had counted on was dry, and so they had to push on late into the night. The cattle, horns clicking as they moved along, bawled pathetically, and every throat in the crew was parched. They did have water, in their barrels attached to the chuck wagon and also in a freight wagon that hauled more supplies, but it was hardly enough for the men, let alone the horses or the cattle.

Jessie told them about another spring. "We'll keep driving the herd all night. I know there is a small stream that we'll find by daybreak. If we keep the cattle moving, it will not be a problem."

The cowboys nodded grimly. They understood that in this sort of a situation there was no alternative but to keep moving, no matter how much their mouths, throats, and tongues swelled, no matter how pathetic the cattle sounded, no matter how their horses began to stagger, no matter how difficult the situation. There simply was no choice.

That night, after more than twenty-four hours without water, was very long. But as luck would have it, at dawn they came upon a small stream, which the cattle raced toward over the last half mile, after catching the scent of water.

"We should stay," Deke Jones said. "We should stay at least until noon. Let the cattle feed a little bit on what grass is here and drink their fill of the water. They're lookin' pretty bad."

"I agree," Jessie said. "We will stay until noon. I'd stay a full day, but we just don't have the luxury of that much time."

"I understand," Deke Jones said. "Come noon they'll be ready to leave. Any sooner than that we'd have to drive 'em from the water."

Jessie knew that was true, and when noon came, the cowboys were able to drive the cattle from the water and then on south. Jessie looked to the distant mountains. She could see a line of peaks that marked the northern boundary of Old Mexico. There were many *banditos* along this southern border, and they were less than fifty miles from it. Down in this country there were no Texas Rangers to protect them. Everyone was on his own, and Jessie knew that there were many in these parts who would go to any lengths to steal a herd of this size and value.

"I think," Jessie said later that afternoon, "we should do a little more night driving and perhaps seek shelter and rest in the canyons during the hottest hours of the daytime."

"Good idea," Ki said. "I'll pass that on."

That night they did keep moving, and they continued to do so in the days that followed. At the end of the week Jessie and the crew were feeling much better. The drive was going well, they were at least halfway to Corpus Christi, and there was more and more grass.

"I think we're going to be all right," Ki said one evening as they huddled around a camp fire. "I think the worst is behind us."

"I hope so," Jessie said. "I really do."

Ki looked at her sharply. "You don't sound as if you believe it."

"I don't," Jessie said. "The closer we get to the coast, the more danger there is from marauders, rustlers, and *banditos*. You know that as well as I do."

"True," Ki conceded. "I do know that, but at least we are through the worst part of the country."

"Yes," Jessie said, forcing a smile. "We need to remind ourselves of that, too."

Jessie did remind herself of that all the next morning and afternoon. She was still telling herself about how lucky they

19

had been, when that evening they saw, off in the distance, a lone rider. Ki studied the rider, and everyone looked to the samurai because his eyes were especially keen.

"*Bandito*?" Jessie asked.

"No," Ki said. "Kiowa."

"Kiowa," Jessie repeated, and then sighed. "Where there is one, there are others, and they are always hungry."

"Yes," Ki said.

"I'll give them beef," Jessie decided.

"One beef, two beefs, then they'll want more," Ki reminded her. "They'll want the herd."

"That's too bad," Jessie said. "They cannot have it."

Ki was silent for a minute, then said, "They'll have it if there's enough of them. They'll have it no matter how much blood is spilled. A thousand head would feed a lot of Indians. Or they can be sold for a great deal of money."

Jessie stared at the lone Kiowa rider. He was perhaps two miles distant, on a ridge, watching them closely. She knew he was a scout, and she assumed that he would soon vanish and that others would then appear to create trouble.

"We'll just have to pray they are only a few," Jessie said. "If there are just a few they will take one or two head and that will be the end of it."

"True," Ki said. "We'll just have to wait and see."

That night Jessie posted double sentries on the herd. The night passed quietly without incident. But in the morning, as soon as they left, Jessie looked to the south, and she and the cowboys saw many, many Indians. Her heart fell. Without the shadow of a doubt the Kiowa would attack her men and try to take this herd. That meant more cowboys would die—maybe they would *all* die before this day ended.

★

Chapter 3

The Kiowa held back all day and that night, Jessie did not sleep. Neither did Ki or the Circle Star cowboys. At dawn Jessie knew a decision had to be made. "This is not a good place to stay and defend ourselves in case we are attacked," she said. "It would be better if we continue on south; hopefully, we can find a better place to fight."

So they got the heard moving just after daylight and continued on. By mid-morning the Indians had moved closer and Jessie had a clear view of them, though they were still a half mile distant, flanking Jessie and her men on the ridges.

Ki said, "I estimate at least fifty Indians. We haven't enough men to stand up against that many. Look! They're coming now."

And they were. Even as Ki spoke, Jessie watched as the Kiowa began to ride down from the hills. When they were a quarter of a mile distant, Jessie ordered the herd to be circled by the cowboys. Everyone was very tense waiting to see what the Kiowa would do. It was clear now that they were heavily armed and that was a bad sign.

"Look!" Ki said.

Jessie already saw that four Kiowa had detached themselves from the main body and were riding forward, slowly. "Let's go meet them and see what they want."

Ki's face reflected disapproval, and Jessie knew that he would have preferred she remain with the herd. But Jessie was determined to be the spokesman for her own herd. Deke, Ki, and one other cowboy, named Paul Beecher, who was chosen to join them, rode out to meet the four Kiowa.

The Indians focused their attention on Jessie. She stared right back at them, ignoring how their eyes boldly took in her figure and long hair. Jessie could see desire on their dark faces, but outwardly she managed to look calm and composed. When they drew within twenty-five yards of the Indians, Jessie raised her left hand and said, "Peace, my friends!"

The Indians registered no reaction to her greeting. Moments passed slowly. Paul Beecher cleared his throat, and his hand slipped closer to the gun at his side.

"No!" Ki said. "If you go for that pistol we'll all be dead!"

Beecher's hand moved away from his holster. The Indians continued to stare. Finally the one in the center, a tall man with red ocher and black streaks across his face, said in broken English, "Beefs! Want beefs!"

Jessie nodded and raised her hand again, with five fingers, indicating that she was willing to give them five of her cattle. But the leader of the Kiowa shook his head violently. He raised his own hand and began to flash the fingers up and down. Once—twice—three—four—five. Jessie lost count. It was clear as the fingers moved up and down that the Indian wanted hundreds of her cattle. This was unacceptable. She could not possibly meet her contract in Corpus Christi or help James Stanford if she had to bargain away very many of her cattle.

"No!" she said with determination.

The Kiowa's round face flushed darkly. The fingers stopped moving and the hand became a fist. He looked to one side, at his companions, and then to the other. "Many beef!" he said, turning back to Jessie. "Kiowa take all beef!"

For a moment there was absolute silence, and then Ki said, "Kiowa die!"

All four of the Kiowa reacted about as Jessie might have expected. Their faces flushed with anger, and as one reached toward his knife, Jessie drew her own gun, cocked it, and pointed it at the warrior. "Go away," she said. "I give you five beefs and you go away."

Jessie turned slightly and yelled back over her shoulder, "Bring us five beefs!"

"Five beefs!" Deke shouted. "Miss Starbuck wants five beefs! Bring good ones!"

Jessie kept her gun and her attention focused on the Kiowa, but she could hear cowboys back in the herd, as they cut out five good beefs and drove them forward. The cattle, once so independent, now seemed loath to separate themselves from the rest. They kept trying to dodge back into the herd. They bawled and were obstreperous until the cowboys finally had to rope them and drag them forward.

When the men finally separated out the five cattle, Jessie indicated that they were to be given to the Indians. She said, "Give them your ropes."

The cowboys nodded. Their faces were strained and pale. They rode forward a little, and when they were near the Indians, they indicated that the Kiowa were to take the ropes. Instead, one of the Indians raised a Winchester repeater and shot all five beefs where they stood, one after another. He was good with the rifle and shot each longhorn directly through the heart. The animals fell, bellowing and kicking.

When the sound of the rifle fire had rolled into silence, Jessie nodded her head, then reined her horse about and returned to her herd. The samurai and her cowboys waited, just in case the Indian with the repeating rifle might decide to unload on them.

But he did not, and soon the Kiowa fell upon the five fallen beefs and began to butcher them on the spot. The hungry Indians made fires as Jessie and the cowboys hurriedly drove the herd away from them.

"Let's move them on as fast as we can," Jessie said.

The longhorn steers didn't like being rushed. They became ornery and unruly, but the cowboys pushed them hard that afternoon. There was not a man among them that did not look constantly over his shoulder, expecting at any minute to see the Kiowa come racing up on their backtrail.

"Five beefs won't satisfy them very long," Ki warned. "They'll be hungry by tomorrow afternoon when their beef bones are finally picked clean."

"I know that," Jessie said. "Tomorrow afternoon we'll be another fifty miles farther south. If we can keep this herd moving we won't even stop at sundown. We'll just push them as hard as we can and hope for the best."

Paul Beecher, a thin, taciturn man, overheard Jessie's words. "Miss Starbuck," he said, "ain't no way we can keep this herd one step ahead of those Injuns. It might take two days, or even three, but those Kiowa will overtake us and next time they won't settle for five. They'll want five hundred!"

Jessie knew that Beecher was right. But she also knew that every mile closer to Corpus Christi was one mile closer to safety.

"Tomorrow," she said. "We'll start looking for a good place to make a stand."

This seemed to satisfy her companions, and the word was soon passed among the cowboys that they would drive all night and tomorrow start looking for a defensive position.

This seemed to raise everyone's spirits, and that night, even though they all were bone tired, they had no difficulty in keeping the cattle moving. The night passed very quickly, each of them wrapped in his or her own dark thoughts, wondering if they would see yet another sunset.

Jessie could barely hide her concern for the cowboys. She had already lost Johnny, and she knew the chances were very good she would lose other good men. But these cowboys knew the dangers of their profession and that the history of cattle ranching in Texas was one of bloody struggle. Jessie also knew that it wasn't her fault that the Kiowa had showed up or that Johnny had died. She was just doing what had to be done—delivering cattle to a market and hopefully benefitting an old family friend.

Early next morning, Jessie looked toward Ki almost instinctively, knowing that he, among all the others, was the one that she could most count upon. Ki was unlike any other man she had ever known. His hair was long, straight, black, almost shoulder length. He wore a braided leather band to keep it in place. He preferred a loose-fitting samurai costume over the traditional Western dress. He also preferred sandals or moccasinlike footwear over boots. In this way he could move very freely.

Ki was often misjudged to be Chinese. In fact, he was not Chinese at all. His father had been an American seaman who had journeyed to the Far East, met a beautiful Japanese lady, and fallen in love with her despite her family's strong objections. As Ki had explained several times, in Japan all foreigners were considered to be inferiors. Ki's mother was ostracized by her family after defying their order not to marry a foreigner. Shortly after Ki's birth, his father died—and his mother, who was now totally alone died of a broken heart soon after.

This had left Ki alone and unfriended. His early years were

filled with pain and suffering. Being half-Caucasian, he was ridiculed and persecuted. He nearly starved as a homeless waif in the streets of Japan. He had been beaten often, and his body still carried the scars. When he was about fourteen, he was almost killed by older boys who drove him from their midst.

Fortunately, an old *ronin* named Hirata had befriended Ki. *Ronin* in Japanese means "wave man," and a *ronin* was called this because he had no master. He was unattached like the waves on a storm-tossed sea, moving here and there without purpose. To be a samurai and then a *ronin,* because your master had died, was one of the worst things that could happen. A *ronin* was an outcast just as the mixed-blood Ki was. He had no master to serve, and the entire point of being a samurai was to serve a master.

Hirata saw in the young half-breed boy something special, and took him in. He was rough and abrupt, impatient, and at times very demanding, but he was also fair. He fed Ki and took care of him and protected him from his persecutors.

Jessie knew that over the years a strong bond had formed between the old *ronin* and the young half-breed boy. Through Hirata, Ki learned all the skills of a samurai warrior. He learned how to use the ancient weapons, including the *katana,* which was the long sword, and the *shuriken,* or star blade weapon.

Ki was particularly adept at using star blades. They were extraordinarily dangerous, and he could throw them with great accuracy, just as a man might throw a knife. There were other unusual weapons that Ki had mastered after countless hours of practice. His bow, for example, was highly out of the ordinary, and it never failed to draw attention because of its shape. When an arrow took flight, the bow would turn one hundred eighty degrees, to face the archer. It was light colored and made of sanded layers of wood.

The layers were glued together and wound at several points with red silk thread. The bow's core was held between two pieces of bamboo that had been tempered by a special fire treatment.

Jessie had seen Ki use the bow many times. She, like all who witnessed it, was amazed at the bow's flexibility, its lightness and strength. Ki could fire arrows with great speed and accuracy. In fact, there was a style of archery that the Japanese called *inagashi,* in which the bowman could unleash fifteen arrows as rapidly as any man could fire a Winchester rifle.

There were other weapons that Ki excelled in using. One was the *nunchaku,* which was two sticks of varying length, attached together at one end by a few inches of braided horsehair. Ki would hold onto one stick, swirl the other around, and deliver a numbing blow. When pressed together, these sticks could also be used to crush a man's wrists or hands. Ki also employed the *surushin,* which was a six-foot length of rope with leather-covered steel balls attached at each end. Jessie had seen Ki use the *surushin* in battle. It was a devastating weapon.

Now, however, as they hurried south, fleeing from the Kiowa and seeking a place to make their stand, Jessie thought twice about all these samurai weapons. Despite the fact that she had seen Ki use them many times in close combat, she wondered if perhaps he would have been better off to have mastered the use of a Winchester rifle, or even a Colt revolver, such as she wore on her shapely hip. But, she thought, none of this matters now. What matters is simply to survive in order to reach Corpus Christi.

At sunset they came upon a place that all agreed would be a good defensive position. It was on a small level plateau where the herd could be easily contained among rocks, from behind which Jessie and her men could fire downward in all directions. Additionally, this little plateau contained a spring that bubbled profusely from the depths of the Nueces Plateau.

"This is where we'll make our stand," Jessie said. "We will keep the cattle here for the night and see if the Kiowa attack at dawn."

Dawn came slowly over the land, and they were all surprised and relieved to see that the Kiowa, while camped only a short distance away, were not forming for an attack.

"What do you suppose they're waiting for?" Jessie asked.

"They're probably trying to wear us down," Ki said. "Maybe they'll follow us a few more days, and then attack. They certainly know that we are a long way from civilization or help. They're in no hurry. They have been well fed. They've probably smoked some of the beef and have enough to eat. They might even have a few beeves of their own somewhere back in those hills."

One of the Circle Star cowboys, overhearing this story, said, "Miss Starbuck, I'd just as soon get this over with and attack them. If we gotta fight, then let's start the party ourselves."

Jessie shook her head. "No," she said. "We're not ready yet."

"What do you mean we're not ready?" the cowboy protested. "This is as good a place as we'll ever find to make a stand. We should just stay right here. We've got water, grass, and everything we need."

"Except time," Jessie said. "Sooner or later we'll run out of grass. Sooner or later they'll sneak up on us in the night, stampede the herd, and take us."

"Then what are we supposed to do?" the cowboy argued.

"We're going to do what we came to do," Jessie said. "We'll continue on south and hope that we can find an even better place to defend ourselves."

The cowboy started to protest, but when Ki placed his hand on the young man's shoulder and squeezed it, protest died in the cowboy's eyes. His chin dipped up and down several times, and he said, "Yes, ma'am, Miss Starbuck. Whatever you say." Ki released his shoulder, and the cowboy walked away, trying not to show his pain.

"You hurt him," Jessie said.

"He needed a small lesson in manners," Ki said. "He will shake it off in an hour or two."

Jessie said nothing. She knew that Ki would not abide anyone arguing with her and that he considered it his role to discipline those who might overstep their bounds.

Within half an hour they were back in the saddle, moving the herd southwest toward Corpus Christi. All day long the Kiowa shadowed them. At times Jessie saw that the Kiowa would sit down and have a meal. They would quickly build a fire, and she knew that they would do little more than sear the beef that she had given them. The Kiowa were patient, just like most Indians Jessie had met. They were more patient than the whites, and they would bide their time until every-thing seemed to be in their favor. Then they would attack.

"We need to find a good place to defend ourselves tonight," Ki said. "I have a feeling that tomorrow they'll run out of beef and attack."

"I have the same feeling," Jessie said. "We'll start looking from this moment on."

They were in luck. For the second time they came upon high ground, this time heavily timbered. There was some grass and a small stream. It was almost a perfect place and the cowboys' spirits rose immediately. Jessie was pleased to see their smiles, and she felt it was her place to say a few words.

Moving among them, she raised her hands for a moment to catch their attention and then said, "Men, I know things have been tense. I know we've had a hard trip, but it will get better. I just have a feeling that if we can survive these Indians, perhaps even pay them a few more beeves in order to continue on into Corpus Christi, everything will be all right. What we need to do is to keep our wits about us, not panic, get as much rest as we can, and always be alert. If we get through this night without incident, I'm quite sure that tomorrow morning we can negotiate with the Kiowa again and things will be worked out."

All the Circle Star cowboys seemed very eager to accept this as truth, and that night Jessie took a small risk by reducing the number of sentries so that while they were protected, the men got more rest. She knew that if they had to fight tomorrow, they would need to be fresh.

Ki, however, had his own plan. "I'm going out to visit their camp."

"No!" Jessie exclaimed. "Please stay here with us. We need you."

But Ki shook his head. He took Jessie's arm and led her aside. When they were alone, Ki said, "Jessie, you know as well as I do that those Indians will attack tomorrow morning." Jessie said nothing, and Ki continued. "The only thing to prevent them from overrunning us is to steal their pony herd."

"What!" Jessie exclaimed.

Ki managed a small smile. "You heard me. I'm going to go in and stampede their ponies and drive them off as far as I can. When I return we will move out. Without ponies the Kiowa cannot overtake and attack us. If I am able to drive the ponies far enough away, then we will see them no more."

"Drive the ponies around to the herd and we'll continue on with them," Jessie said. "In that way, they cannot recapture them and ever come after us."

"That's kind of what I had in mind."

30

Jessie sighed, "I don't suppose you will allow me to come along with you tonight?"

"No," the samurai told her, as he stepped over to his saddlebags and removed his *ninja* outfit. Jessie knew what this meant. The *ninja* outfit was black and included a hood. In Japan the *ninja* was the most feared of all the warriors— in fact, the word meant "invisible assassin." A *ninja* could move so stealthily and so quietly, and blend himself in with the surroundings so well, that he was almost impossible to detect. He could look like a tree or part of a wall or bushes, or whatever, until he came within striking distance of his intended victim. Once there, the *ninja* was always lethal, for he must kill his intended victim or lose his honor.

As Jessie watched Ki slip on his *ninja* costume and pull the hood over his head so that only his eyes showed, she felt a sense of building apprehension. "I wish there were some other way."

"There isn't," Ki said softly. "Don't worry. I will return with the Indian ponies and we will rid ourselves of this threat."

Jessie believed the samurai because he had never failed her and she was sure that he would not do so now. "If I lost you . . . " she began slowly, groping for words.

Ki reached up and touched her cheek. "You won't. This is what I have been trained to do. I am samurai and I am *ninja,* and everything will be fine."

A moment later Ki disappeared, not heading directly toward the Indian camp, but circling to the north. He moved with swiftness and grace, and within an hour he had covered almost eight miles in a broad circle that brought him up behind the Kiowa camp. The Kiowa were not expecting anything. Their camp fire was huge, and they sat around it laughing and talking and eating the last of the beef that Jessie had given them.

31

Ki sat under the dark shadow of a tree for perhaps an hour, studying them closely while making his plans. When he was satisfied that he had seen all the Kiowa that were coming and going out to the horse herd, he moved back into the shadows and circled around a little farther until he came to the edge of a small meadow where the Kiowa ponies were being held.

Some of the ponies were down sleeping, while others grazed quietly in the darkness. Because there was a three-quarter moon, Ki could see them all. He waited, watching the sentries until he was sure he had them all in place, and then he moved forward toward the nearest one. Ki had counted four sentries—two of them at the far end of the meadow and two of them at this end. He did not anticipate a problem, and as he moved closer, the Indians were completely unaware of the impending danger.

Ki stepped up behind them, moving low and quickly, then before they even suspected his presence, the *nunchaku* flashed in the moonlight, cracking softly against the skulls of the two Indians and dropping them like stones. Ki stepped over them, satisfied that they would not quickly awaken. He moved back into the forest and circled around to the other end of the meadow.

The second pair of sentries presented a little more of a problem because they were farther out in the meadow, and thus more difficult to reach without being seen. Ki lowered himself in the grass and slithered forward like a snake, making no sound whatsoever. Had there been a dog, perhaps he would have been detected, but as it was, he was able to come up almost next to the unsuspecting Indians. As he suddenly rose from the ground, his hand flashed and caught one of the Indians in a *tegatana* blow right at the base of his skull. The Indian grunted softly and fell.

The second Indian just had enough time to open his mouth to scream a warning, but before the warning erupted, Ki was on the man, knocking him down, slashing with his hand. Two blows and the Indian was unconscious. Ki stood up. He took a deep breath and then moved toward the horse herd, walking with determination. Once he was among the herd, he reached into his *ninja* costume and removed from a large pocket a rope bridle.

"Easy now," he said to a fine-looking bay gelding. "Easy now." The animal snorted at Ki's unfamiliar scent. But Ki was so relaxed in his actions that the animal did not spook or run away. Ki quickly had the bridle in place. Then he swung aboard the animal and quietly began to drive the entire pony herd away. The horses moved off readily enough, and when they were about a mile from the Kiowa camp, Ki began to make clucking sounds with his tongue, causing the ponies to run.

Far behind him, Ki thought he heard shouts from the Indian camp, and he suspected that someone had discovered the fallen sentries and realized that the entire pony herd was missing. Ki began to shout and yell and quickly drive the horses forward. It was dark and dangerous, and Ki prayed that his horse did not take a nasty fall. He pressed close to the animal, his fingers wrapped in mane, and drummed his heels against the bay's ribs.

A few of the horses had circled back, but most of the pony herd seemed entirely willing to run ahead of him. Ki continued shouting and waving, and with the warm night air in his face, he felt good.

The Kiowa ponies ran on and on. Ki let them run until they were so exhausted they began to slow down; then he gathered them up into a closer band and, slowly, steadily, began to drive them to where he was sure to intercept the Circle Star herd.

Dawn came suddenly on the land, and Ki was very pleased when he saw the Circle Star longhorns emerging from the sunrise to greet him. Jessie came racing forward, a wide smile on her face. "I knew you could do it!"

Ki said nothing, but he was pleased. He was even more pleased when he saw the happy smiles of the Circle Star cowboys and vaqueros. Without a word, he drove the Indian ponies in among the Texas longhorns and they continued on south.

Chapter 4

For the next three days the Circle Star crew moved steadily down off the Nueces Plateau, and they began to feel that the threat of danger from the Kiowas was past. However, late one afternoon as they were moving through a narrow, rocky valley, shots suddenly rang out from both sides. One of the cowboys screamed and toppled from his saddle, and his death was quickly repeated by two more riders.

"Take cover!" Jessie shouted. "Take cover!"

None of the cowboys had to be told. Diving from their horses into the rocks, they took defensive positions as bullets screamed in at them from the hidden ambushers. The herd began to run, but Jessie and the cowboys paid them no attention.

"How many?" Jessie asked Ki as the samurai crouched beside her.

"I can't tell. But more than seven."

A bullet careened off the rocks beside Jessie, splintering rock into her arm and causing blood to flow.

"Stay down," Ki said anxiously.

Jessie ducked. "We're in a bad position. They are above us and they've got us pinned down. The cattle are moving away. Perhaps they're trying to separate us and the cattle in order to steal the herd."

"No," Ki said. "There aren't enough of them. I'm sure there are only six or seven all together. I imagine they're the ones that were sent to recover their stolen ponies."

"So, what do we do?"

"We wait," Ki said. "We stay down low."

Another Circle Star cowboy cried out in pain and collapsed. Jessie scooted over to his side. He had been shot in the shoulder and the blood was flowing freely. She tore a rag from his shirt and began to bandage the wound. "You're going to be all right," she said.

He looked up at her, eyes glazed with pain. "I don't know," he wheezed, bubbles on his lips. "I think I got it through the lung."

Jessie looked at the man, and she was afraid the man was correct. She could hear the wheezing, wet, sucking sound as he tried to pull breath through the wound.

"Just hang on," she pleaded.

He looked up at her and nodded. She tried to make him comfortable as the bullets continued to pin down her cowboys.

"There is nothing we can do," Ki shouted to the others. "We must just stay low and wait."

"But the herd!" one of the cowboys protested. "They're scattering!"

"I don't care about the cattle," Jessie said. "Not when it comes to your lives."

Jessie looked up to see that the Kiowa had not only been firing upon her men, but also her cattle. She quickly counted almost two dozen longhorns that had been killed outright, and another four or five that were staggering around, badly

36

wounded. "Maybe," she said, "there is enough beef here to finally satisfy them."

Two hours later, the cowboy who had been shot through the lung died. It wasn't a pretty thing to watch as he struggled, gasping for breath, and finally drowned in his own fluids. Jessie railed in silent fury at the injustice. "We'll take him along with us and bury him as soon as we can," she said.

"We can't take all our dead," one of the cowboys said.

"Yes, we can," Jessie insisted. "We'll take every single one of them just as soon as it's dark."

And that's what they did. They gathered up their dead, and as the moon rose higher in the sky, they moved out from behind the rocks and slipped on down through the valley and out farther onto the plains. When they found their horses, they slung their dead across the saddles, climbed on behind and rode on after the herd. It was nearly daybreak when they finally managed to gather the cattle.

Once again, in the early morning, Jessie held a ceremony as they buried their dead. As she looked back toward the valley of death that they had traveled and that had proved such a loss to them, Jessie said, "I hope we have seen the last of the Indians. We're getting close to Corpus Christi. It can't be more than a hundred miles."

A cowboy said, "The way things are going, it might as well be a thousand."

Jessie ignored the remark. She looked at Ki and he nodded with understanding. Then, leaving the graves behind and gathering up the herd with the few men that remained, they started south again. The days that followed were difficult, but uneventful. Now that the cattle were in good grass country, all they wanted to do was stop and graze, and Jessie's heart went out to them. Yet, she did have a deadline to meet and there was a constant danger in this part of the country.

"We have to keep them moving," she said. "I know they

are hungry, but we must not let them stop."

"They can graze around Corpus Christi," Deke Jones said.

"Yes," Jessie said. "I think they'll have at least three or four days—maybe a week. Sometimes those ships can be late."

With that said, they continued moving on, following the river, fattening the cattle as best they could, and keeping a watchful eye out for more Indians.

One morning Jessie recognized a lightning-burned tree and said, "I remember seeing this years ago. We can't be more than fifty miles from Corpus Christi now."

The cowboys grinned. One of them said, "I can almost smell the salt sea air."

"Yeah," another said happily.

The mood became elevated. Once again the cattle settled down to a routine, and as they slowly fattened along the grassy trail, they became easier to work. But then, two nights out of Corpus Christi, all hell broke loose.

It happened about four in the morning. Jessie was sound asleep, Ki was somewhere else camped by himself, when suddenly the samurai shouted a warning and came racing into camp. He had barely reached camp when Jessie heard the thunder of horses' hooves and wild screams. She rolled out of her blankets, as did her cowboys, and dove for cover, reaching for her gun.

The next few minutes were sheer terror as a large band of cattle rustlers came charging through camp, firing blindly in every direction. Some of the Circle Star cowboys foolishly stood up and fired back, and the flashes of their muzzles cost them their lives. Jessie and Ki knew better. They stayed down low and slipped away in the darkness. It was all they could do. To stand and fight would have meant instant death.

The next two hours seemed to last forever, as they slowly worked their way up into the rocks, hearing the cries of dying men and the sound of receding gunshots. When the first gray light of dawn appeared on the eastern horizon, Jessie and Ki stood up, both shaken and feeling rage and helplessness.

"I guess we had better go down there," Ki said. "Maybe there are some who survived."

"Don't count on it," Jessie said bitterly.

When Jessie and her samurai returned to their camp, there wasn't a single living Circle Star rider left. A few Circle Star cowboys might have managed to grab their horses and flee to save their lives, but Jessie doubted it. Two or three men were missing, but all the rest she could account for—every single one of them dead, shot numerous times.

Jessie fell to her knees, her lips pulled back from her teeth, and she clenched her fists in anger. "I swear," she cried, "I swear by all that is holy I will find those that did this and they will be held accountable! No matter where they've taken the herd, no matter how far they've gone, we will find them and exact our vengeance!"

Ki helped Jessie to her feet, and they stood wearily, almost leaning against each other as they surveyed the destroyed campground, the overturned chuck wagon, the death and destruction. "Who," Jessie asked, "who could have done this? *Banditos*?"

"No," Ki said. "It wasn't *banditos*, nor was it Indians. I heard them. They were Americans."

"And where will they take my herd?"

Ki shook his head. "I don't know. Maybe Corpus Christi, but probably down into Mexico."

"Yes," Jessie agreed. "That's where they would go. To Mexico. And that," she added, "is exactly where we shall also go."

"We need to bury the dead, gather up what we can, hope we find a few horses, and then go on."

"There won't be any horses," Jessie said. "Those cattle

rustlers will have taken every last horse they could find, including Sun and your horse, Ki."

"Then—"

Jessie cut Ki off. "Then we will walk," she said. We will walk and not stop walking until we find that herd and those who are responsible for stealing it. Then we'll find guns and a way to kill them."

The samurai studied Jessie. He had been with her before when she was in a vengeful mood like this, and he knew that she meant business. Jessie was not one who lost her temper easily, nor did she hold a grudge, but when it came to her cattle and her cowboys, Jessie was a tiger. She would stand and fight, and before the dust was settled, Ki knew that either they or the cattle rustlers would all be dead.

★

Chapter 5

Jessie and Ki followed the trail of the cattle all that first day. The rustlers had turned south, leaving the Nueces River and heading into another barren, semi-arid area where travel was difficult. The sun blistered down on their heads, and by the second day Jessie and Ki were almost weaving for lack of water.

"There must be some up ahead somewhere," Jessie said wearily. "They can't take the herd much farther without water." The samurai nodded and they kept moving.

Early that evening they did come upon a pond, where the rustled Circle Star cattle had stopped and drank their fill, then spent several hours. Jessie and Ki found the water polluted by the herd.

"They must have ridden on ahead with their canteens or water skins," Ki said. "They filled them up for themselves and then they let the cattle in, knowing that they would foul the water for anyone who tried to follow."

Jessie nodded. "The Apache and the Comanchero have been known to do the same kind of thing. What do you suggest we do?"

"We have to stay," he told her, "until the water clears. It might take a day and we can, of course, strain a little through our handkerchiefs."

They spent a full day waiting for the cloudy water to clear, and then they drank their fill. Fortunately they had canteens, which they filled.

As they prepared to leave, they saw a lone figure approach from the south. He was riding an old Mexican burro, and the burro was braying noisily as it trotted down from the dusty hills toward the water. "Hello, there!" the man cried, waving his hand cheerily.

Jessie and Ki exchanged glances. Ki said, "Who do you suppose this might be?"

"I have no idea," Jessie said. "But he looks harmless enough."

"Don't be too sure of that," Ki said as the old man on the burro came riding in closer, shouting and laughing. "He looks a little crazy to me."

"Well, well," the old man said, slipping off the back of his burro and doffing his hat to reveal a shining baldpate. "If it ain't a couple of pilgrims out for a nice walk." The old man looked at each one of them and then guffawed heartily.

Jessie and Ki remained impassive and when the old man's laughter died, the samurai said, "Who are you and what are you doing way out here by yourself?"

"My name is Pablo Smith," the man announced rather grandly, "and I am a soldier of fortune . . . an adventurer . . . a storyteller . . . a man of the world . . . an ally that you can count on." And with that he winked.

Jessie had seen many of this type of man. They thought much of themselves and talked a great deal, but when it came to action, they were all smoke and no fire.

"My friends," Pablo said, measuring Ki and Jessie, "I can

tell that you have fallen upon hard circumstances indeed."

"We've had a little trouble," Jessie admitted. "We're trailing a herd of my stolen cattle."

"Oh, yes," Pablo Smith said. "I have seen those cattle and they are gone."

There was a moment of silence. Finally Jessie said, "What do you mean they are gone?"

"Just what I said, ma'am. Your cattle are gone. Herded onto the buccaneer ships bound for South America."

Jessie stared in stunned silence, wondering if this strange, crazy-looking man could possibly be telling her the truth. "If that is so, Pablo, describe my brand."

"Circle Star," Pablo Smith said. "Circle Star indeed. And I know you. You are Miss Jessica Starbuck. I've heard about the Circle Star Ranch. Those were fine cattle, ma'am. A little thin, but don't you worry. Them people down in Guatemala and Central America'll just eat 'em up without hardly noticing."

Jessie looked at Ki, who just shrugged his shoulders. "Mr. Smith," Jessie said, "are you sure my cattle have already been loaded onto buccaneer ships?"

"That's right, ma'am. Happens to a lot of herds. Probably a herd a week, comin' in from Brownsville and Matamoros from up in Texas. That's where they're bought and sold, yessir, and then loaded on the buccaneer ships like yours were, ma'am. Anyhow, once they're on them ships, they never come back. Why I would expect your cattle would be halfway to South America by now."

"Damn!" Jessie swore. Then she looked up at the crazy old man. "Do you know who bought or sold my cattle?"

Pablo Smith scratched the side of his whiskered cheek. His beard was silver, as were his eyebrows and what was left of his hair. His nose was a red bulb, his face was as dark as oiled

43

leather, and he was missing several teeth and two fingers on his right hand.

"Well, ma'am, could be I know and could be I don't know."

"What is that supposed to mean?" Jessie asked.

"Just what I said. I may know and I may not know. You see," he said, winking mischievously, "sometimes a few dollars or pesos will lubricate a man's mind a little. Know what I mean, ma'am?"

Jessie knew exactly what he meant. She reached into her jeans and found a roll of money, and while Pablo Smith watched with wide-eyed expectancy, she extracted several dollars. He reached for them, but she drew the money back, and Ki stepped in between them.

"Mr. Smith," Ki said, a faint threat in his voice, "I wouldn't be too anxious to grab for that money again."

He bristled. "Oh, is that right? What are you gonna do to try and stop me?"

Ki said nothing. He folded his arms across his chest, but he did not move from in front of Jessie.

"Mr. Smith," Jessie said, "I really think that you ought to consider what Ki has just told you. I don't mind paying for advice, but I have to be sure that it is at least correct and complete."

Pablo stepped aside so that he could look at Jessie. "Miss Starbuck," he said, "I heard a lot about your Circle Star Ranch and about the fine way you treat your cowboys. Most everything I heard about you and your father is good. Now you don't really think I would be stupid enough to try and cheat someone like you, do you?"

"I'm not sure."

"Well, I wouldn't," Pablo Smith said with indignation.

"My apologies," Jessie said. "I'm just being careful." She stepped forward and extended the money, which Pablo Smith took, counted very carefully, and placed in his pocket while a small grin grew at the corners of his mouth.

"Well, ma'am," he said, "you pays handsomely. Yes, ma'am, you really do. Now about them cattle of yours. I know the man that took 'em and he knows me. In fact, I have sworn to kill the son of a bitch."

Jessie blinked. "Kill him?"

"That's right. His name is John Coburn and he is one of the most evil people you have ever seen in your life. Worse than any Apache. Why, he up and killed my partner, Ben Turpin. Old Ben and me prospected and worked these hills, caught wild mustangs and generally raised hell around these parts for more than thirty years. Yessir, and there were times when we did strike gold and had money in our pockets. The last time," Pablo Smith said, his voice dropping and his face growing hard, "John Coburn found out about it and his men shot Ben dead."

"I'm sorry to hear that," Jessie said quietly.

"They shot him down in cold blood. Old Ben had stolen my share of the money, of course," Pablo said, "but what he didn't drink he would have given back. Point is, he had the money and John Coburn and his men shot Ben down. That's why I swear I'm going to kill that man some day."

That said, Pablo slipped his hand into the pack lashed to his burro. He produced a bottle of tequila, uncorked it with a pop, and held it out to Jessie. "Here you go, ma'am. It's a hot day."

"No, thank you," Jessie said.

"No?" Pablo asked curiously. "Well, I'll be damned! What about you, Chinaman?"

Ki bristled. "I'm not a Chinaman. I'm half-American, half-Japanese. There's a big difference."

"Well, hell! You've seen one slant-eye you've seen 'em

45

all," Pablo said, ignoring the way Ki's eyes flashed as he raised the bottle of tequila and drank his fill. He corked the bottle and squinted at Jessie.

"Ma'am, if you need help to find John Coburn and the men that stole your cattle . . ."

"You can find this Mr. Coburn for me?" Jessie asked.

"Why, hell yes!" Pablo Smith exclaimed. "He don't take no pains to hide. You can find him in Matamoros raisin' hell or just across the border up into Brownsville. You ever been to either one of them places?"

Jessie shook her head. "I've been in most of Texas but never down in that part of the country."

"Well, ma'am," Pablo Smith said with a shake of his head, "they're hard places. And I have to tell you right now that a woman with your looks might be in serious trouble."

Jessie patted the six-gun on her shapely hip. "I can take good care of myself, Mr. Coburn. And when I cannot, Ki is more than capable."

Pablo looked at Ki without much confidence. "He ain't big enough to whip the likes of Coburn and the sort that run with him, and he don't look a bit mean."

"Well, he may not be mean, but he's plenty capable. Tell me, Pablo, how much money would you charge to lead me to this John Coburn?"

"How much money you got?"

"I'll pay you ten dollars."

"Ten dollars! Is that all? Why—"

"All right," Jessie said, "twenty dollars."

"Hmmm," Pablo mused, stroking his jaw again. "Now we're starting to talk some business."

"How far," Ki interrupted, "is Matamoros?"

"Oh," Pablo Smith said, "maybe a hundred miles, give or take ten or twenty."

"Then that's where we should go," Jessie said.

Pablo held out a callused, dirty paw. "Money first."

Jessie paid the man, and although she would have preferred to depart that evening, Pablo said that he and his burro were plain tuckered out. So they spent the night and left early the next morning, angling south toward Matamoros and Brownsville along the Rio Grande.

Pablo proved during the journey that he was a man of good nature and unfailing high spirits. He whistled and sang old songs despite the heat, dust, and the dog tiredness they all felt, and after a few pulls on his bottle, he liked to do a little shuffling jig and talk about the wild days of his youth.

"Yes, ma'am, I was a mountain man," he said. "I traveled with Jim Bridger and Jedediah Smith and some of the greatest mountain men that ever trapped in these Western streams. I seen the Yellowstone and the Smokey Waters, and I trapped all the way over into California. I was there when Hugh Glass stumbled in after bein' half et to death by a bear, and I led many an immigrant wagon train across this dry, hot country. I fought Apache, Kiowa, and Cheyenne. And I whupped 'em all!"

Jessie and Ki exchanged glances.

"Well, it's true," Pablo Smith exclaimed with indignation. "And I trapped beaver in all the rivers of the West until they finally was cleaned out. Then, I took up huntin' buffalo. Yessir, I did. I was one of the best buffalo hunters Kit Carson ever knew, and he'd tell you so if he was alive."

"I'm sure you were," Jessie said tolerantly. "It sounds like you have had quite an interesting life."

"Well, I have. Good days are all gone," Pablo said. "Ain't nothin' but the leavings now around the West. Too many people, that's the problem with everything. Too many

47

damned people. Why, to get a little solitude now a man has to go down into Mexico."

"There's plenty of solitude left in Texas," Jessie said. "It's still a big country. Lots of open land for the claiming."

"Lots of open land?" Pablo scoffed. "Why, the land that's left free and clear ain't worth havin', 'cept when there was buffalo here, wild cattle or horses. No, sir! Can't grow anything, there's not enough water, wouldn't support a jack rabbit, is what it wouldn't do."

Jessie chuckled. "There are men that will come, families and homesteaders, too, who would differ with you on that opinion, Pablo, but anyhow, what concerns us now is John Coburn. How many men usually ride with him?"

"Oh, it depends," Pablo said. "Sometimes a hundred. Sometimes not near so many."

"A hundred!" Ki asked, skeptically.

"Why, sure. When he raids down into Mexico, he might take a hundred men. And if he was goin' up into the Texas country, far up there where there's Texas Rangers, he might take a hundred men. On the other hand, sometimes he just likes to take a few friends and go out and raise a little hell— maybe steal a few head of cattle, a few head of horses, even a good lookin' woman, or a kid he can sell down into Mexico or Central America."

"He sells women and children?" Jessie asked, trying to keep from sounding shocked.

"That's right," Pablo said. "He'd sell anything he can to make a dollar."

"What else can you tell us about him?" Ki asked.

"Well, sir," Pablo said, "I could tell you he's big. Stands, oh" —Pablo raised his hands above his head as high as he could reach—. "Stands about that tall." Pablo lowered his hands and spread them apart. "About that wide."

48

"That's the size of a grizzly bear," Jessie said.

"Yep, that's about as big as he is and he's about as hairy, too. Women seem to like him though. He's always got a couple of 'em on his arm when he's in Matamoros or Brownsville. Likes to drink, likes to dance, likes to kill people. I think most of all he likes to make money."

Ki had listened to this in silence. "Are there others that do this sort of thing in this country?"

"What sort of thing?"

"Steal cattle," Jessie said. "Or raid in Mexico and take women, children, and horses."

Pablo scowled. "Used to be a lot of 'em, ma'am. But John Coburn has already shot most of his competition. And he's got plenty of friends hangin' around those border towns, stealing, looting, and killing. They pay him a little money on the side. But Coburn is the worst one of them all."

Jessie shook her head. "What about the law? Hasn't anyone tried to stop him? To arrest him?"

Pablo chuckled and scoffed. "Hell, ma'am, you don't know John Coburn! He's got half of northern Mexico and half of southern Texas afraid of him!"

"I'm not afraid of him," Ki said.

"Well, that just means then that you're a fool, Chinaman."

Ki reached out and grabbed the old man by the shirtfront. "I told you," Ki said in a tone that left little doubt of a warning, "I'm not a Chinaman and I don't appreciate being called one. I am a samurai!"

"A what?" Pablo asked, eyes suddenly wide with concern for his health.

"A samurai!" Ki said, releasing the old fool. "A samurai is a Japanese warrior. I have been trained to use my hands and feet in fighting."

"Your hands and feet!" Pablo might have laughed, except

49

Ki had shaken him up a little bit. "Mister, ain't no hands or feet ever stood up against a man with a gun or a knife."

"Ki can," Jessie said. "But that's not the issue right now. We need to find Coburn."

"I'll take you to 'im, like I said. But once you find him, if you let him know you're after his hide, he'll kill you real sudden-like—if you're lucky. Of course," Pablo added, looking Jessie up and down, "with a woman as good lookin' as you are, I imagine Coburn would probably decide to keep you for himself. Understand, Miss Starbuck, that there are a lot of women in Texas and Mexico who'd be mighty pleased to belong to that hairy giant."

"Well, I'm not one of them," Jessie said. "All I want is to bring that man to justice and to be reimbursed for my herd. It's bad enough that I've let my friend Jim Stanford down, because I'll have to make up for that, too."

"Well, I don't know any Jim Stanford," Pablo said. "All I know is if you find Coburn you're findin' trouble."

Jessie thought about that many times during the next few days as they traveled south. She learned from Pablo that Matamoros and its American neighbor, Brownsville, had an interesting and rather violent history.

Matamoros had first been settled in 1765 and then burned twice and pillaged many times after by the Apache and various pirates and raiders that had come from their ships plying the Gulf Coast. Later, during the Civil War, Matamoros had prospered handling contraband cotton, smuggled out of the United States by Confederates for shipment to European markets.

Across the Rio Grande, Brownsville had profited during the war just as well. Originally it had been called Port Brown and had been built by the United States in order to enforce its claim that the Rio Grande was its southernmost border. Brownsville had often warred with

50

its neighboring Matamoros across the border, as both the American and Mexican communities had vied for dominance. Brownsville's greatest distinction was that it was the site of the Civil War's last battle, at Palmito Hill. Ever since that time, the plots and counterplots of revolutionaries on both sides of the border had kept Matamoros and Brownsville in a constant state of agitation.

"Brownsville is a city," Pablo said, "famed for its lawlessness because so few sheriffs outlive their inauguration. Yes, ma'am, there is a killin' almost every night in Brownsville, and if there ain't, then Matamoros will pick up the slack. Hardly a day goes by that the mortician ain't loadin' some stiff into his wagon and takin' him out to the cemetery."

"How interesting," Jessie said cryptically.

"Yes, ma'am, if you're cravin' action and excitement, Brownsville and Matamoros are the places to be. And if you're really cravin' to die young, Coburn is the man to meet."

Jessie said nothing. She was sure that Pablo was exaggerating, and yet she knew that it was very likely that she was heading straight for big trouble. However, she had lost a thousand head of cattle, and most importantly, her cowboys had been murdered by Coburn's ruthless cattle rustlers.

When they finally reached the outskirts of Brownsville, Jessie saw a bustling, sunbaked city very close to the Gulf of Mexico. There were trees, gardens, and a big plaza. It looked inviting from a distance, but Pablo had advised them that they should not be fooled.

"It looks plenty peaceful from a distance," he warned. "But once you get down there among 'em—"

"I know," Jessie interrupted. "It's a hard, and dangerous, border town. But all I want you to do is to find Coburn,

51

and we'll take care of the rest."

"Maybe," Pablo said as they moved on down toward the city, "you should consider hiring some gunfighters. There's always plenty in Brownsville."

Jessie shook her head. "They're not the kind of men that I want."

"They may not be the kind of men you want," Pablo snorted, "but they're the kind that might keep you alive. And you could hire 'em cheap. A dollar a day is the goin' rate. You get forty or fifty of those gunslicks, find Coburn, and riddle him to pieces. Then it would be over and you'd have won."

Jessie sighed. There was no use in trying to explain to Pablo that what she really wanted was to bring Coburn to justice. If she did that, maybe others like him would decide they had better go straight.

"Oh," Pablo said, "one more thing I should tell you."

"What's that?"

Pablo looked at Ki and then at Jessie. "You should know that Coburn is an expert with a Bowie knife. He likes to cut folks up. So, if he draws his knife, you best clear out in a hurry, just like everybody else around him will do."

"I'll remember that," Ki said, reaching inside of his cloak to finger his own *tanto* blade knife.

As they entered Brownsville, Jessie was worried. She had to admit that Pablo's warnings had left her apprehensive. However, there was no turning back. Justice had to be served in this lawless border town, and the very thought that Coburn was actually capturing people and selling them as slaves made her blood run cold. As Pablo explained it, Coburn could do this because he was in cahoots with a ruthless band of buccaneers.

"Their leader is Luke Lafitte."

"Luke Lafitte?"

"That's right," Pablo said. "He claims to be a descendant of the famous buccaneer Jean Lafitte."

"He *was* famous," Jessie said. "Whatever happened to him?"

Pablo sighed. "It's a long story, ma'am, and rather a sad one. You see, Jean Lafitte and his buccaneers and pirates settled on Galveston Island and lived there for many years in peace as a pirate colony."

"I see," Jessie said.

"Well, after a while, though," Pablo said, "the young men grew stronger and Lafitte weaker until he couldn't control his colony. The young pirates began to raid up and down the Gulf Coast as far over as New Orleans. Finally, the United States warned Jean Lafitte that if he couldn't control his men, they would all be attacked and driven off Galveston Island."

Jessie had heard part of this story before, but she wanted to hear Pablo Smith's version, so she remained silent.

"Well, sir, Lafitte gathered up all his law-abiding citizens and he told the young pirates they would have to stop raiding up and down the Texas and Louisiana and Mexican coasts. And, of course, they refused because they were getting rich. So what happened was, Lafitte took his loyal friends and loaded them on three ships, then he sailed away. He left them bloody pirates on Galveston Island and it's from them that Luke Lafitte was sprung."

"The bad element, huh?" Jessie said.

"That's right! He's the one that buys the slaves and stolen cattle from Coburn."

Jessie said, "It's a ruthless, bloody business that needs to be smashed."

"Oh, it's ruthless and bloody all right," Pablo said, "but you two poor, worn-out gringos ain't about to do nothin' to smash it. It'll live long beyond you and someday, when old

53

Coburn is dead, somebody else'll just step in and take his place."

"Maybe," Jessie said, as they entered Brownsville, "but that doesn't mean we shouldn't do the best we can to end it once and for all."

★

Chapter 6

After reaching Brownsville, Jessie, Ki, and Pablo found hotel rooms. They were weary and tired, but agreed that the first order of business was to learn Coburn's whereabouts.

"We should start in the saloons," Ki said. "I'll see what I can find out."

"Hell!" Pablo growled. "They see a Chinaman like you comin' and it'll cause nothin' but trouble."

"Then come along with me," the samurai challenged.

"All right, I will."

"Be careful," Jessie said, as the pair left the hotel room. "Be real careful!"

"We will," Ki promised.

During the next hour Pablo and Ki visited one saloon after another. In each they would sip a beer or whiskey, then move along, all the while looking and listening for news of John Coburn. In one particular bar Pablo suddenly stiffened. "Over there!" he said. "See that man?"

Ki followed Pablo's eyes. "The tall one?"

"Yeah. He rides for John Coburn."

"Then let's go and meet him," Ki said.

They moved over beside the man, ordered drinks, and pretended to chat without any interest, until finally Pablo said, "Evenin', Joe."

Joe Fisher looked up at the old man. "Who are you?" he asked.

"My name is Pablo Smith. Don't you know me?"

"No," Fisher said. "Am I supposed to?"

For a moment Pablo said nothing. He just stared at the man until Fisher grew slightly uneasy.

"What are you lookin' at, old man?"

"Nothin' special," Pablo said. "I was just wonderin' if perhaps I could buy you a drink."

Fisher's face registered surprise. "Why would you do that? You don't look like you have enough money to buy yourself a drink."

"Oh, but I do," Pablo said, raising his glass of tequila. "I have a little money. You should not judge all men by their looks."

"Why not?" Fisher said. "I can tell that you're poor, that you have nothing and never have had anything."

"That isn't true," Pablo said. "Once I was actually a fairly wealthy man. I had gold."

"Come on, now!" Fisher said as Pablo signaled for more tequila.

"It's true. I had gold," Pablo insisted. "I had a friend, a partner, who found gold not one hundred miles from here. Lots of gold."

"Hell," Fisher snorted with derision, "everybody tells that story."

Pablo waited until the drinks were brought to them. "I suppose." He took his tequila in his hand and raised it to toast Fisher. "I didn't expect you to believe me. The thing I was wondering is that I used to know a man named John Coburn, and I understand that you know him too."

56

Fisher's eyes narrowed a little. He sipped his tequila, pursed his lips, and sipped some more.

"Do you know him?" Pablo asked after a long silence.

"Yeah, I know him," Fisher said. "What of it?"

"I simply have a need to speak with him."

"About what?"

"Just about this and that. Maybe some cattle, maybe some gold."

"You're a crazy old man," Fisher said. "I don't think I want to talk to you anymore."

Pablo tossed down the rest of his tequila and signaled the bartender, who came over. Pablo reached into his pocket, retrieved some money, and laid it down on the bar. "Leave the bottle this time," he said.

The bartender nodded, scooped up the money, and left the bottle of tequila. When Fisher replaced his glass on the bar, Pablo refilled it and said, "There is no reason to be suspicious of me, is there? After all, I am but an old man. A man who has never had anything. And besides, I may be able to help Coburn."

"You help John Coburn?" Fisher scoffed. "Mister, your kind is as common in this country as ticks on dogs. You got nothin', you're worth nothin'. You can't help Coburn."

"You could be wrong," Pablo said, refilling their glasses. "In fact, you *are* wrong. I do know where there are some cattle to be found. Good cattle."

"Oh, sure," Fisher said, drinking more. "There are cattle scattered all over Texas, and there are cattle up in the north, and there are cattle in Mexico. There are cattle everywhere."

"Ahhh!" Pablo said. "But these cattle are close, tame, and can be herded. And, you can make some money."

"If that's true, old-timer, then why don't you get some of your friends to steal the cattle and sell them yourselves?"

Pablo saw that Fisher's leering face was filled with mirth.

57

"You mock me," he said. "But I'm telling the truth, and I think Coburn would be very unhappy with you if I tell someone else about these cattle."

"You know him?" Fisher asked.

"Yes," Pablo said. "I have dealt with him before."

Fisher drank in silence for a few minutes. "Where are these cattle? Tell me where they are, and then I'll decide if I'll tell Coburn."

"No," Pablo said. "That is not good enough. I need to tell him myself."

"Then what's in it for me?"

"There may be something. That will depend on Coburn. It is good to do a favor for a man like that, eh?" Pablo asked.

Fisher nodded. "Yes," he admitted, "it is good."

"Then will you take me to him?"

There was a long pause. "Tomorrow," Fisher said at last. "I will take you to him. Do you have a horse?"

"No," Pablo said, "but I have a burro."

"A burro!" Fisher scoffed. "You couldn't keep up with me. We have many miles to go."

Pablo shrugged. "I would not be coming alone. Besides, I can find a horse."

Fisher's eyes narrowed. "What do you mean you would not be coming alone?"

Pablo turned to Ki, who was pretending not to listen. "This man," he said. "He is my friend. He would come with us. He has some money."

Fisher studied Ki closely. "He looks like a Chinaman. Chinamen don't have any money."

"This one has money," Pablo insisted. "This money to buy the tequila—I got it from him."

"Who is he?" Fisher asked suspiciously.

"Just a friend. Just a man who knows where these cattle are."

58

"Then you don't know?" Fisher asked.

"I know, but so does he."

"Hell!" Fisher growled, refilling his glass and then tossing it down. "You're talking in riddles, old-timer."

"These cattle," Pablo said, sensing that he was losing Fisher's interest, "there are perhaps five hundred. They are fat. They are unbranded. They are as easy to drive as sheep. I think they would bring a good price."

"All right," Fisher said at last. "Tomorrow morning. Nine o'clock. Outside this saloon. But you got to have a horse, and so does your friend. And if there is any trouble or you try to deceive me, then you'll be shot, either by me or by Coburn."

Pablo felt a chill because he knew this was not an idle threat. And yet his face did not betray his fears. "There will be no tricks," he said. "Just an old man and a Chinaman. That is all."

"Fair enough. Now, why don't you ask your friend to buy us some more drinks?"

Pablo motioned to Ki, and when the samurai joined them, Fisher said, "Who are you and what do you want?"

Ki was prepared for these questions. He looked Fisher straight in the eye and said, "I know a man with cattle. I have worked for him, and he has cheated me. Now I just want a little something."

"Aha!" Fisher said with a half laugh. "Now I begin to see. You want revenge!"

"I want justice."

"Good," Fisher said, completely satisfied now. "Justice. Revenge. It's all the same depending on who's looking at it from what angle. We leave tomorrow."

Ki nodded and forced himself to taste the awful tequila.

Early the next morning, Jessie was awakened by a knock at her door. "Who is it?" she said, sitting upright.

"It is Ki."

Jessie climbed out of bed, dressed quickly, and went to open the door. She let Ki inside and then closed the door. The samurai looked tired. "Ki, you didn't get much sleep last night, did you?"

"I had enough," Ki replied. "We found a man who is willing to take us to Coburn."

"You did!"

"Yes. We are leaving this morning. There isn't much time. We have to buy horses."

"I'll give you some money," Jessie said, reaching for her saddlebags. "And did you find out how far away Coburn is hiding?"

"No," Ki said. "But the outlaw is so feared in these parts that I doubt he's hiding much at all. I think he might be living in Matamoros."

"I wish I could go with you," Jessie said. "I *should* go with you."

"No," Ki said. "We will be back by this evening, and then we will make plans."

"Please be careful!"

"Don't worry," Ki replied. "I will."

"Do you trust Pablo?" Jessie asked suddenly.

"Yes," Ki said, hand on the doorknob. "He does nothing for free, but I believe that he is a man of honor. I don't think he's setting us up for a trap."

"I'm relieved to hear that."

When Ki left, he went directly to the nearest livery and purchased two good horses, saddles, bridles, and blankets. The horses were quickly saddled. Ki mounted one and led the other back to the saloon. He tied them both in front of the saloon and settled back to wait.

Pablo showed up at about eight-thirty, and they talked idly for a few minutes until Fisher appeared.

"Did you get any horses?" Fisher asked, his eyes very bloodshot from a night of hard drinking.

"We did," Ki said. "We're ready to ride."

"Well, I'm not," Fisher said. He banged back through the saloon doors and went inside. Ki walked over to the doors and watched as Fisher demanded a bottle of whiskey. When his request was denied because he had no money, Ki entered the saloon and paid for a bottle.

"Thanks!" Fisher said gruffly, as he snatched the whiskey from the bar, glared at the bartender, and then stalked outside. "Now let's get the hell out of here!"

Ki and Pablo Smith mounted their horses, and a few moments later Fisher came riding up. He was slightly drunk and in a foul mood. "Let's go!" he said gruffly as he sawed on his reins and spurred his horse hard down the street, causing it to break into a gallop.

Ki and Pablo also put their horses into a run as they galloped out of Brownsville, toward the Rio Grande. When they reached its wide, muddy banks, Fisher did not hesitate, but drove his horse into the warm water, which was only a few feet deep. "Stay right behind me," he yelled, "there are patches of quicksand in here."

They crossed safely, then skirted Matamoros. Fisher kept his horse at a steady trot as Ki and Pablo followed through the heavy brush. There was no point in asking how far they were going. All was clear now that John Coburn and his band of cutthroats were somewhere down in Mexico, probably within a few hours' ride.

It was almost noon when they topped a low sagebrush-covered hill and gazed down into a small valley that fed down to the coast. There they saw a hacienda, not unlike many that could be found in Mexico, and distinguished only by the large number of sturdy corrals.

"This is it," Fisher said. "Come on!"

61

Ki and Pablo exchanged glances, and then the old man held back for a second and said, "I think I've changed my mind. I'll be leavin' now."

"What!" Ki said.

"Coburn would kill me," Pablo said. "He knows I'd try to shoot him on sight for killing my pardner, Ben. I'm leavin'!"

Before Ki could say anything more, Fisher turned around in his saddle and yelled, "What the hell's the holdup back there?"

"The old man has got cold feet," Ki said.

"Jesus Christ!" Fisher shouted, reining his horse around and spurring back to them. "What the hell do you mean, got cold feet!"

"I didn't tell you the whole truth," Pablo said, looking both scared and ashamed. "I'm not exactly on the best terms with Coburn."

Fisher reached for his gun. Yanking it out, he waved it at both Pablo and Ki. "What the hell is up with you two!"

Ki shook his head. "I have no idea! But I do know where this herd of fat cattle is just waiting to be rustled. As for the old man, I don't know what the problem is."

"Well, we're going to find out," Fisher said, cocking the hammer of his gun. "You two ride on ahead of me. Old man, if Coburn wants your hide, then he'll have it and I'll be the one he'll thank."

"Please," Pablo said, his voice quavering with fear. "Let me go! I've done nothing except give you free tequila. Let me go back to Brownsville."

"Nope. I brought you into Mexico and now I'm going to take you to Coburn's camp down there in the valley below us."

Pablo laced his fingers together and raised them in supplication. "Please!" he said again. "He'll kill me!"

"You're past your natural time, anyway," Fisher said derisively. "You've already lived too long."

With that, Fisher motioned them forward so that Ki and Pablo Smith had no choice but to continue down into the valley.

Ki could see many saddled horses tied to a long hitch rail before an old hacienda made of adobe. There were a few trees and dozens of chickens running free in the yard. In the corrals were perhaps three hundred head of cattle.

As they rode down to the hacienda, Ki's mind raced. He knew they were in serious trouble, and that he'd gotten into something he might not be able to survive.

★

Chapter 7

By the time Ki and Pablo reached the front of the hacienda, there was a good-sized crowd of hard-looking men watching them suspiciously.

"What you got, Joe?" a heavyset man growled. "A couple of strays you hauled in?"

"You bet," Joe said, dismounting. "Where's Coburn?"

"Oh, he's inside," the man said, drawing his pistol. "I'll call him out."

At the sound of the gunshot, John Coburn appeared to fill the doorway. The giant was even bigger than Ki had expected. Coburn was at least seven feet tall, broad-shouldered and heavily muscled. He had to duck when he came through the doorway, and close at his side was one of the most beautiful Mexican girls Ki had ever seen. She could not have been more than eighteen years old, with large brown eyes, bare feet, and wearing a simple cotton dress and a beautiful turquoise necklace around her neck.

"What you got there?" Coburn said, and then before anyone could answer, a wide smile creased his lips. "Well, I'll be damned! If it ain't old Pablo Smith. Son of a bitch! I've been lookin' to skin your hide for almost five years now."

Pablo, like Ki, had not dismounted and his hands were clenched to the saddle horn. "I been looking to settle the score with you, too. So why don't we stop this fiddlin' around and settle this between us?"

For a moment there was a strained silence, and then John Coburn said, "Hell, old man, you really think I'd stoop so low as to fight someone like you?"

"With guns or knives," Pablo said, "I'd have a chance."

"The hell you would," Coburn sneered. He glanced sideways at Ki. "Who are you?"

"My name is Ki," the samurai told him, "and I have heard that you pay good money for cattle."

"Oh, I pay money all right. I don't know how good it is. How many cattle you talkin' about and where?"

Ki paused. He did not want to tell Coburn anything more than was absolutely necessary, since there really was no herd. "About five hundred cattle," Ki said, "less than three days' ride from here. Easy enough to take—hardly guarded at all. Broken to trail drive."

Coburn studied him closely. "Who owns 'em?"

"I'd rather not say," Ki told the outlaw leader, "until I've been paid."

"Oh, you'll be paid all right," Coburn said. "Pull him down, boys."

A second later Ki and Pablo Smith were jerked from their saddles and rudely shoved forward until they stood looking up at the outlaw. Coburn studied each of them for a moment.

"Old man," he said, "I think I'll just have a noose put around your neck and have you hauled up in the air by that big old tree. I'll enjoy watching you kick and choke. With any luck the show will last for five or ten minutes."

Pablo paled a little, but said nothing. Coburn turned his attention to Ki.

"Who the hell are you, Chinaman?"

Ki remained calm and patient. "Like I said, I know of a herd that would be good pickin'."

"Where is it? Who owns it?" the giant demanded.

Ki stood his ground. "If I told you now, then you wouldn't need to pay me. Right?"

A tall, muscular, cruel-looking man said, "Why don't you let me teach him a lesson in manners?"

Coburn looked sideways at the man. "All right, Jess."

Jess stepped forward and at the same instant drove his fist into Ki's ribs. It was a powerful punch, so hard that it actually lifted the samurai off his feet. The samurai staggered, and Jess kicked at his knee. Ki saw the blow and managed to reach down and grab Jess's boot. He jerked it straight up over his head, and the brawler went down hard. Someone swung at Ki and hit him in the side of the face. He staggered. Another man grabbed him, spun him around, and drove a fist into his belly. Ki's knees buckled.

Coburn shouted, "Leave him alone, boys. It's between him and Jess."

Ki shook his head, trying to clear his vision. Fortunately for him, Jess was also dazed. When the brawler finally climbed to his feet, he balled his fists, lowered his head, and charged. The samurai was ready. As the man came in, Ki used a snap kick, and it caught Jess in the crotch. The outlaw screamed in agony, and the iron-hard muscles of the samurai's hand slashed downward and struck Jess's shoulder. The man staggered, but did not go down.

Ki stepped back. He glanced at the giant, wondering what would happen next. He could not read Coburn's thoughts, but the outlaw leader was eyeing him strangely. "Come on, Jess," someone shouted, and then the chant went up and everyone began to shout for Jess. Ki waited patiently. He could have stepped in and finished Jess off, but Ki sensed that he needed

66

to give the man the edge so there would be no question about the fact that he had whipped him fairly.

Jess kept dragging in air. He shook his head until it was finally cleared, and then he pulled a knife from his boot top. Ki tensed. He looked at Coburn, but the giant said nothing. Ki began to move backward slightly, and a wide smile crossed Jess's lips.

"Chinaman," he said, "I'm gonna carve you up like a Christmas turkey."

Ki had faced men with knives before, and he knew how dangerous they could be. He feinted with his left hand, as if to strike, and Jess swung with the knife. Ki ducked under Jess's arm, grabbed it, and brought it down hard across his knee. A terrible scream filled Jess's throat as his arm snapped. Ki whipped his elbow back and slammed it into the man's throat, abruptly ending the scream.

Jess's eyes bugged. His face grew red as he struggled and gagged for air. Ki stepped back and very methodically punched the man in the face, knocking him down. Jess landed hard. He rolled twice, still gagging. Several men grabbed him and tried to help as Jess's face slowly turned purple.

Ki met Coburn's hard, unforgiving eyes. "He won't die," the samurai said, "but neither will he want to fight me again."

"Who the hell are you?" Coburn asked.

"I'm a samurai," Ki said.

"Come inside."

Ki nodded his head, then looked to Pablo, who had remained motionless during the fight. "What about him?"

Coburn shot a hateful glance toward the old man, then looked at one of his lieutenants. "String him up by his thumbs."

But Ki shook his head. "No, he is my friend. We're in this together."

"Then you'll die together."

67

Ki started to say something, but Pablo interrupted. "Ki, there's no sense both of us dying."

Ki weighed the circumstances carefully, then looked at Coburn and said, "We're in this together. We have a herd of cattle that we know will be easy pickin's. If you string him up and kill him, you'll have to do the same to me."

Coburn's eyes widened with surprise. "What the hell is Pablo to you?"

"He's a friend."

"And you're willing to die for a friend?" Coburn asked with disbelief.

Ki shrugged. "I think you're too smart to kill him."

There was a long moment of silence, and then the girl standing beside Coburn looked up and said, "Please. Spare the old man's life. He's going to die in a few years anyway."

Coburn frowned. Ki could almost read the giant's thoughts. The outlaw leader did not want to appear weak before his men. He had issued an order, and he dared not give the impression that a Mexican girl could change his decisions.

So, Coburn's face darkened. He reached back his hand and slapped the girl hard. She staggered. Her eyes filled with tears of pain. "It is still wrong to kill the old man!" she cried.

Coburn raised his hand as if to strike her again. The girl raised her chin defiantly. "Go ahead. Hit me if it pleases you."

"Damn!" Coburn said lowering his hand. "Conchita, sometimes I don't know what the hell gets into you."

She said nothing, and at that moment Ki knew that this was a girl with great strength and courage.

"All right, samurai," Coburn said, dismissing her. "Come on inside and let's talk about those cattle."

"What about my friend?" Ki asked, resolved not to let the outlaws make cruel sport with Pablo. "Is he in or not?"

"Bring him along!" Coburn snapped. "But if he steps out of line just once I'll have him drawn and quartered. He'll die slower than if the Apache was having fun with him."

Ki looked at Pablo, who nodded his head with understanding and followed Ki into the outlaw's headquarters.

The hacienda was cool and dim inside. It was also littered with bones, dried food, dirty dishes, old saddles, and unwashed clothes. The place reeked of decay and badly needed a good airing out, but Ki said nothing.

"Sit down!" Coburn ordered the two men.

Ki and Pablo found chairs and sat across from the outlaw leader. Coburn slapped the sofa beside him, and Conchita came quickly to his side. "All right," Coburn said. He threw his arm around the Mexican girl and nuzzled her neck before he said, "Where the hell is this herd you came to tell me about?"

Ki weighed his next words carefully. "The cattle, as I said, are up north, not far away. They'd be easy to find and are broken to the trail. It's quick and easy money for all of us."

"How many?"

"Five hundred," Ki repeated, "and they're in good condition."

Coburn's eyes narrowed and his voice sounded a warning. "If this is a trap of some kind, you'll both die."

Ki nodded. "We understand. How much will you pay?"

"Your cut will be a dollar a head," Coburn said quickly. "That's what I pay everyone."

"And you'll sell them for how much?" Pablo asked.

"Shut up, old man!" Coburn bellowed. "How much I'll sell 'em for is none of your business!"

Ki was afraid the old man might lose his temper and get them both killed, so he said very quickly, "We'll take it. Five hundred dollars. Half now and the other half when you get the herd."

"Bullshit," Coburn sneered. "You get paid when I get paid."

"And when would that be?" Ki asked.

"When we deliver the herd to my friend's ships. You understand that?"

Ki nodded. "Where will the cattle go?"

Coburn leaned forward. "Samurai, that's none of your damned business."

"They go down to Central and South America," Pablo said.

Coburn shot an angry glance at the old man. "You always did have more mouth than common sense."

"I know where all the stolen cattle that come through Matamoros are sold," Pablo Smith said.

Coburn shrugged. "So what! All you should be interested in is the money you are going to be paid."

"We can leave tomorrow morning," Ki said, desperately wanting to get Pablo away from the outlaw leader before he exploded in anger and violence that might get them both killed.

"Good enough."

"What about tonight?" Pablo demanded.

"Tonight you'll be locked up."

"Locked up?" the old man snorted. "How the hell come? What do you think I'm goin' to do? Slit your throat?"

It was the wrong thing to say. The giant stood up. He walked over to the old man, grabbed him by the shirtfront, and then slapped him first one way and then the other. Pablo tried to reach for his knife, but Coburn knocked it away and punched the old man in the face. Ki almost winced because the blow was so powerful, and Pablo was already unconscious before he struck the floor.

Coburn swung around, and Ki could see that the giant's blood was up. "You got a problem?"

70

"No," Ki said.

The giant relaxed. He glanced over at Conchita. "Why don't you bring the Chinaman and me some tequila?"

Conchita disappeared. She returned a few minutes later with a tray, bottle, and two glasses. She poured the glasses half-full and handed one to Coburn and the other to Ki. Ki preferred not to drink strong spirits, but in this case, he made an exception.

"To a profitable deal," Coburn said, raising his glass.

Ki raised his glass and took a sip of the tequila. Its fire burned his mouth, and then when he swallowed, his throat. He placed his glass down hard on the table. "To money," he said.

Coburn nodded and took Conchita's hand. He called to his men, and two of them entered the room. Coburn pointed to Pablo Smith. "Drag the old bastard to the guardhouse. Put the Chinaman in with him."

"With pleasure," one of the men said, coming over to grab the samurai.

Ki stepped back and raised his hand slightly in a fighting posture. "I can walk by myself."

The man nodded and looked at his leader as if asking him a question. "It's all right," Coburn said. "Like the Chinaman said, he can walk to the guardhouse himself. Just carry Pablo Smith."

Ki realized he was staring into the eyes of Conchita. There was something in her expression that he wanted to read, that was just for him alone. But before he could figure it out, he was rudely shoved around toward the door and marched outside and across the yard, toward an adobe hut. It had a strong wooden door and heavy latches.

Ki was roughly pushed inside, and a moment later, Pablo, still unconscious, was hurled inside as well. The door slammed shut, plunging them into darkness. Ki heard the lock turn outside, and then one of the men chuckled before walking away.

The samurai quickly circled the room, his fingers brushing lightly across the interior surface. Even before his eyes became accustomed to the dim light, Ki learned that the walls were made of adobe. Had he a few days, he was sure that he could scrape and cut his way through. But since he would be called upon tomorrow morning, there was no chance of escape.

Ki reclined in the darkness. He tilted his head back to gaze up toward the thin, strawlike shafts of light glancing down through the darkness. He was hungry, he was cold, and he had no idea how he was going to get out of this mess.

Pablo's breathing was irregular, and Ki hoped that the old man hadn't sustained serious injury.

"What are we going to do now?" Ki asked out loud. "How are we going to get out of this mess?"

But Pablo, being unconscious, had no answers, and so the samurai closed his eyes and put his mind in a different place. A place of peace and tranquility and, above all, hope. A place where Ki knew his mental and spiritual strength would be renewed. He had no idea what he would do tomorrow when Coburn and his men saddled up and rode out to find the imaginary herd that Ki had promised to show them. But he would worry about tomorrow, tomorrow. Right now, it was enough simply to rest and to gather one's thoughts in preparation for whatever would happen.

Ki fell asleep, his thoughts mostly concerned about Jessie Starbuck, who would, even now, be back at the hotel fretting about him. He wished there were some way he could get word to her of his dire circumstances, but then again, perhaps it was better that she did not know.

Ki slept soundly that night and decided early the next morning that he would somehow have to locate a herd and play the situation out to the end. If he could find a herd and it could be stolen without bloodshed, then driven down to the Gulf of Mexico Ki was sure the trail would end with buccaneers under Lafitte. After that, Ki could return to Jessie and she would know what to do.

Ki heard Pablo groan and saw him stir. "Are you all right?" the samurai asked.

Pablo mumbled something. Ki knelt beside the old man, put his forefinger and his thumb on each side of Pablo's jaw, and wiggled it slightly.

"Ouch!" Pablo cried.

"It's not broken," Ki said. "It's probably just a dislocation. You took a tremendous punch."

"Leave me alone."

But instead, the samurai used both hands, and with a quick jerk, he manipulated the jaw. Pablo cried out again, but a few minutes later he was working his jaw just fine.

"What the hell's going to happen now?" Pablo asked glumly as he rubbed his eyes.

"We've got to find about five hundred good cattle and rustle them without killing anyone in the process."

"You're out of your mind," Pablo said. "We'll never find a herd."

"Yes we will," Ki replied. "We'll find one. Maybe we'll just have to ride a little farther than we told Coburn."

"If we ride too far we'll never return."

The samurai was silent for a minute. He knew that Pablo was right and that there was little margin for failure. If the outlaw leader even began to suspect that this was a trick in order for Jessie to seek justice and repayment for the loss of her Circle Star cattle, then the giant would kill them.

"Pull yourself together," Ki said, helping the old man to his feet. "They'll be coming for us soon, and before they do, we had best get our story straight."

Pablo stood up and leaned against the wall. He shook his head and then rubbed the side of his jaw. "That big son of a bitch hits like the kick of a mule. Don't you cross him, Ki. I know that you're a fighter. I've seen that. But you're no match for John Coburn."

Ki said nothing. The time would come, however, when he supposed he would have to fight Coburn, probably to the death. But until that moment there was no sense even thinking about it. Right now he and Pablo had to get their story straight so that when the outlaws came to put them on horses, they would know exactly what to say and do. Their very survival depended on it.

★

Chapter 8

Ki and Pablo Smith were dragged out of the little block house a little later and, without any breakfast, ordered to mount a pair of waiting horses. Ten minutes later, Coburn stepped out of his adobe, gave the señorita a kiss, and then turned and swaggered over to mount his horse. He motioned for Ki and Pablo to come on up and ride beside him.

"You know where the hell we're goin', I don't. Lead off."

Ki exchanged quick glances with Pablo, and together they rode north. Ki had no idea where he was going or where he would find a herd, but he supposed his best chance of finding one was in the United States. They splashed back across the Rio Grande, circled Brownsville, and rode deeper into Texas.

The sun grew warm during the afternoon, and they kept their horses moving fast. As the morning hours passed, Ki saw no cattle, but he knew that there were herds driven down this way on occasion, and sooner or later they would have to come across one. Finding a herd was not the main problem. The real problem was trying to figure out how he could possibly steal a herd and not have there be some killing.

Ki wasn't at all sure how he would handle it, and when he looked sideways at Pablo, he suspected that the old man was also wrestling with the same question.

Early in the afternoon they stopped and dismounted under the shade of some thickets near a spring. They let the horses drink and they all took short siestas. "It's the Mexican way," Coburn said, coming over to tower above Ki. "I learned that a siesta will allow a man to live longer and feel better. Allow him to enjoy his women more, too," he added with a wink.

Ki said nothing. He simply closed his eyes and pretended to go to sleep. Two hours passed. Flies buzzed, but otherwise, there was no sound in the thickets except the scurrying of an occasional rabbit and the stomping of the horses' feet. When the siesta was over, they remounted and rode steadily through the long, hot afternoon.

At dusk they came upon the first set of ranch buildings that Ki had seen. Unfortunately, the ranch had been abandoned some years before, and as they rode through the yard, Ki could see that it had been put to the torch by Apache. They passed two more burned-out ranches before sundown and camped near a small stream, all of them weary and growing increasingly impatient.

Coburn came over to Ki and Pablo and made sure that their bonds were tight and that they were well guarded. "We're going to find this herd tomorrow, right?" he said, his voice menacing.

"Yes," Ki said. "Tomorrow."

"Five hundred cattle, at least, right?"

"That's right," Ki promised with as much assurance as he could muster.

Coburn seemed satisfied. He relaxed and sat down beside the samurai. Ki noticed that his eyes kept flicking to Pablo, and it occurred to the samurai that Coburn at least respected the old man as a dangerous opponent.

76

Coburn was in a surprisingly talkative mood. "Some day," he said, "I intend to quit this business. I've got some money saved up, and I think it will be about time to step aside for a younger man. I've got several who are ready to take control."

Ki nodded. "You have some pretty rough-looking men."

"It takes rough men to exist in this country," Coburn said. "It's the law of the gun down here, just as it is throughout most of the West." When Ki said nothing, Coburn continued. "I never saw a man fight like you do, with your feet, I mean, and the way you hit with the edge of your hand. Where did you learn all that?"

"In Japan," Ki said, "when I was a boy."

"It's a strange way of fighting."

When Ki said nothing, Coburn continued.

"I never thought in my whole life I'd see a man your size whip Jess. He's a tough son of a bitch fighter. I've seen him break a lot of men. I'm about the only one among us he would never try and tackle, and that only because of my size."

"He's a hard man," Ki said.

"He'll kill you someday," Coburn remarked. "You broke his arm and humiliated him."

"He gave me no choice. Besides, it was a fair fight."

"Yeah, it was a fair fight," Coburn agreed, "but all the same, the next time he won't pull a knife, he'll pull a gun."

"If he does," Ki replied evenly, "I'll have to kill him."

Coburn chuckled. "I'll say one thing for you, Chinaman, you sure don't lack in confidence. But then, hell, neither do I. That's what most of the men who ride with me don't seem to understand. A man has to believe he can do a thing before he really can do it. Most folks are all the time worryin' and doubtin' their own abilities. Not me. Ever since I was young I knew that I was gonna be somethin' special. I was gonna be a leader."

77

"You could join the Texas Rangers," Ki said. "Maybe be an officer in the military."

"Hell," Coburn snorted, "I did join the Confederate Army and fought at the Battle of Shiloh. I was almost killed. I could see what was happening to the Confederate armies, and I fought almost a year before I deserted. I came back down in Texas and found out that folks in these parts don't forgive a deserter. I killed a couple of men who made comments about it and I found my way across the border into Matamoros. In Old Mexico people aren't so quick to judge. Either that or they're smart enough not to say anything."

Coburn turned his attention to Pablo. "How's your jaw, old man? Did I break it?"

"Hell, no," Pablo growled. "You landed a damned sucker punch. I wasn't ready."

"That's your problem," Coburn said. "You must always be ready. You should know that by now. It's a surprise to me that you're still alive."

Pablo seethed, but he said nothing. Ki was glad. He had a feeling that if Pablo sounded off too loudly, Coburn would simply pull his gun and drill the old man between the eyes, and there would be nothing anyone could do to stop him.

"Well," Coburn said, "I guess I'll be gettin' some shut-eye." He stood up and walked to the edge of the firelight. "Samurai, I want you to know that I sure as hell don't trust you. But I'll go along with this game until tomorrow night. If you haven't found us a herd of fat cattle by then, well, it's gonna go hard."

"I understand."

"As long as you do," Coburn said, turning and moving away.

They left early the next day and continued riding all morning. It was almost noon when they finally spotted some cattle. Ki reined his horse in and pointed. "Over there," he said,

78

indicating a few cattle grazing at the mouth of the valley.

"That's part of the herd?"

Ki took a deep breath. He could not see what was farther down in the valley, and if these were the only cattle and he said yes, he knew he was in deep trouble. But if he said no, he wasn't sure that he could stall Coburn much longer.

"I'm not sure," he hedged. "It might be the ranch, but then again it might be a little farther to the north."

"Shit!" Coburn said, "I think that this is a con game all the way. And if it is, you'll both be dead men in another hour."

Ki said nothing and prayed for some luck.

★

Chapter 9

Ki led the outlaws into the valley. At the far end, he saw a ranch. He could see that it was occupied, because there were several horses in the corral, chickens running around the yard, and a dog who took up loud barking when he saw the approaching riders. Ki looked sideways at the rough band of outlaws. He knew that there was little mercy in their hearts and that they would kill the occupants of this ranch without hesitation. He could feel his own heart beat faster as they approached the ranch yard. Suddenly, a puff of gunfire erupted from one of the windows and a bullet sailed just overhead. At the same instant, the door to the ranch house slammed shut, and all of the windows were quickly shuttered.

Coburn drew his horse up sharply. "Hello the house!" he yelled. There was no answer. "Hello the house!" Still no answer. Coburn motioned for his men to split into two groups and circle the ranch house. "If we need to," he said before the men rode away, "we can just ride on around and take their cattle. We don't have to face any bullets."

"We ought to kill 'em," one of the men said. "They damn near killed us!"

"The hell with it," Coburn said. "Let's just get the cattle and what horses we can stampede."

So they began to circle the ranch house, staying just outside rifle range. To Ki's great relief, it was a large herd in good condition. Coburn was obviously pleased. "I was beginning to think you two were just stringing us along," he said.

"Nope," Ki replied. "We sort of enjoy the idea of staying alive."

Coburn chuckled and started to say something, but at just that moment, the ranch house door burst open and four men came charging outside, trying to save the herd. They were gunned down in a hail of outlaw bullets. There was nothing Ki could do at all, except watch. His mouth twisted with bitterness. Then he heard a shout and turned to see an old man begin to hobble out of the ranch house. He had a Kentucky rifle in his hands.

"Goddam you!" the old man shouted, his voice shrill and hysterical. "You ain't takin' our cattle!"

Coburn pulled his Winchester rifle from his saddle boot. He levered a shell into the breech, raised the rifle to his shoulder, and began to take aim.

Ki's arm slammed down on the rifle, knocking it sideways as it exploded.

"What the . . ."

"There ain't no sense in killing him too," Ki said. "Let him be!"

"Let him be!" Coburn screamed, his face mottled with rage. "What the hell do you think he's going to do with that rifle he's carrying? Shove it up my ass?"

"I'll take care of him," Ki said. "We don't need to kill any more people."

Coburn didn't like it, but before he could argue, Ki galloped off fast toward the house. When the old man saw the samurai coming on horseback, he stopped, raised the rifle, and took steady aim, and just as he squeezed the trigger, Ki threw himself from his horse. He struck the ground, rolled, and came to his feet running. It took him less than ten seconds to reach the old man. He slashed downward with the edge of his hand, catching the man at the base of his neck and crumpling him to the ground.

"Stop it!" a voice cried from the ranch house. Ki whirled around just in time to see a girl come racing outside, a percussion pistol clenched in her hand. "Stop it, you hear?"

Ki stood his ground. The girl was tall, dark haired, and about seventeen or eighteen years old. Her pretty face reflected outrage rather than fear. When she drew near Ki, she raised the pistol with both hands, cocked it, and said, "You killed my grandfather, didn't you!"

"No," Ki said, "he's still alive. I saved his life."

"Saved his life?"

Ki turned and pointed toward the rustlers. "Had he come any closer he would have been shot!"

"Don't try and tell me that!" she screamed. "You killed him."

Ki turned and pointed at the old man. "See for yourself. He's still alive—just unconscious. Take him back to the ranch house."

The gun was shaking so violently in the girl's hand that Ki was afraid it was going to go off, and the way his luck had been running lately, she would drill him through the heart.

"Take a look," Ki urged, stepping away.

The girl came forward, and when she reached her grandfather's side, she dropped to her knees and placed her fingers on his neck. "He *is* alive!"

"Of course he is, and if you'll let me take him back inside the ranch house, he'll come around soon."

"I don't understand any of this," she said, the gun still pointed at Ki. "Those men shot our cowboys and now they are rustling our cattle. You're one of them and . . ."

"I'm not one of them," Ki said quietly. "Trust me."

"Trust you! After what you just did to my grandfather?"

"Please," he said, watching as Coburn's rustlers began to gather up the herd and drive them back toward Rio Grande. "Just do as I say."

But Coburn came galloping up. "Well, well," he said, "what the hell do we have here? A pretty woman, huh?"

Ki saw naked desire change the outlaw leader's face as his black eyes undressed the girl. "Leave her alone," the samurai warned.

"Leave her alone? You're telling me what to do?"

"You've got a woman," Ki stated. "This one's mine."

"What!" the girl screamed. "What the hell are you talking about?" She raised her pistol again, and before Ki could move, she fired. The samurai felt the ball whiz past his forehead. He dove to the ground, rolled, and heard her gun explode again. John Coburn bellowed in pain and slumped in his saddle.

"Goddammit! She shot me!" he croaked. The outlaw leader wasn't exaggerating. He had a nasty flesh wound in his upper right arm. Still he managed to drag his pistol from its holster. Ki was sure he would have actually shot the girl, had the samurai not jumped forward and knocked her unconscious.

He stepped in front to shield her from the outlaw's gun and said, "Let me have her! I'll make sure she doesn't do anything like that again."

"I oughta teach her a lesson," Coburn said. "I oughta make her pay for this!"

"Why?" Ki said. "You got your cattle, and all I want is this

83

girl and the five hundred dollars that I have coming."

"You'll get it in hell!" Coburn said, whipping his horse around and spurring away hard.

Ki picked the girl up and quickly carried her back inside the ranch house. He found a pail of water and a rag, then dampened it and used cold compresses on her face until her eyes fluttered open. She started to gasp and struggle.

"Easy," Ki said, "easy. They're leaving."

"But our cattle—my grandfather!"

"There's nothing you can do about any of that now," Ki said.

Her eyes filled with tears. "I won't be your woman!" she cried. "I had a husband. I won't have another."

"Shhh," Ki whispered. "It's going to be all right."

"All right! How can you say that! Everything we've worked for is gone now."

"We'll get your herd back," Ki promised. "I know where they're going."

"Who are you?" she asked, confusion thick in her voice.

"I'm a friend," Ki said simply. "I saved your grandfather's life and I think I probably saved yours. They're far more important than the cattle."

For a moment she just stared at him, and finally she said, "Help me up." Ki helped the girl up. She was strong and full-bodied and courageous. "We best go help my grandfather."

Ki nodded with agreement, and they went to get the old man. When they reached his side, Ki picked the grandfather up and carried him back to the house, and there he again used the damp cloth until he roused the old man into wakefulness. Like the girl, he came awake confused and struggling. Ki had to pin his arms down and keep telling him to take it easy, that everything was going to be all right. When he finally stopped struggling, Ki released him and stood up.

"Your cattle are gone. There was nothing I could do about that. But at least you have your lives and I will try and return your herd."

The old man's face twisted with bitterness. "We'll never see the cattle again, and we'll never see you again. Why, if I had my rifle I'd shoot you right now, just like I'd a shot them others."

"I can understand that," the samurai said. He turned to go and was halfway across the yard when the girl shouted.

"Wait!"

Ki stopped and turned. "What do you want?"

"Where are you going?"

"I'm going after them," Ki said, wondering what would become of Pablo now that the cattle had been found. He was afraid Pablo would not have long to live.

He was just thinking this when, suddenly on the horizon, he saw the old man come galloping out from behind the hills. Ki grinned. Somehow Pablo must have eluded the gang and managed to escape, thus saving his own life.

When Pablo galloped into the yard, he looked excited. He was grinning broadly. "Goddam! I got away! I got away! We're both still alive. I thought you were a goner, Ki!"

"No," the samurai said.

"Who in the hell is this?" Pablo asked, looking at the girl and her grandfather.

"I don't know their names," Ki said, "but it was their herd that Coburn took."

"They're just lucky to be alive," Pablo said. "That's what they should be thinkin' about. Lucky just to have their hides."

"Lucky!" the old man screeched. "Why, goddamn you, I'll whip your skinny ass if you call me lucky! Them sonsabitches took our herd. It took Alice and me two years to round up that many cattle. And what happened to all our cowboys?"

85

There was a moment of silence, and then Ki said, "I'm afraid that they all were shot."

At this news the old man went crazy. He threw himself at Ki with such a maniacal fury, the samurai was forced to knock him unconscious. Pablo dismounted and said, "I'll give the old man this much. He's got some piss and vinegar in him."

"He's got a reason to be upset," Ki said.

"So what are we going to do now?" Pablo demanded.

Ki gave the matter several moments' thought, and while he was doing it, the girl looked up from her grandfather and said, "It doesn't matter what you're going to do. Grandpa and I are going after our herd! They didn't take our saddle horses."

It was true. There were four or five saddle horses still in the corral. The rustlers had been in such a hurry that after Coburn had been wounded, they hadn't bothered to risk taking the corralled horses, several of which barely looked rideable.

"We'll all go," Ki said, "together. I'll help you get your herd back, and there's another person who will help also."

"Who's that?" Alice asked, dampening the rag and wringing it out as she began to gently sponge her grandfather's face.

"Her name is Jessica Starbuck. I work for her."

"So do I," Pablo said.

"Jessica Starbuck?" the girl echoed. "Is she the one that owns the famous Circle Star Ranch?"

"That's the very one," Ki said. "You've heard of her?"

"Who hasn't?" Alice said. "She's famous all over the world, isn't she?"

"Yes," Ki said.

Pablo looked surprised. "Famous all over the world, huh? Well, I'll be damned! I should have asked her for more money."

Ki ignored the remark. "Jessica is waiting to hear from us.

86

She'll want to help and she'll know what to do."

Alice did not look convinced, but since there was no other alternative, she nodded her head. "As soon as Grandfather can ride, we should leave. In a few days the buccaneers will be loading our herd onto their pirate ships, just like they do all the others."

"We lost a herd," Ki said. "That's why Miss Jessica Starbuck is down here. Our entire herd, one thousand cattle, were rustled and all our cowboys were shot. Jessie and I were the only ones who survived. So, that's why we have just as much interest in catching those men as you do."

Alice drew a deep breath. "I don't know who you are or even what to believe anymore. I only know that Grandpa and I can't do this alone, so I'm going to have to trust you."

"You can."

"I hope so," the girl said, as her grandfather roused. "And before Grandpa finds his rifle again, I think we'd better tie his hands together until he simmers down."

"Good idea," the samurai said, moving over to the old man and then pulling his hands gently around behind his back and tying them. "He sure is a humdinger."

"Grandpa's tough," Alice admitted. "After my husband died, he and I teamed up together. I'm as good a hand as most, and it's taken us a long, long time to get this many cattle together. We had just hired those four cowboys a few months ago and we were about to brand."

"Don't worry," Ki promised, "we'll get your cattle back."

The girl did not look convinced, but her attention was fixed on her grandfather. Ki moved off to join Pablo. He stared into the distance, toward the receding dust cloud where the herd had vanished.

"We were lucky," Ki said.

"I know that," Pablo replied quietly. "Both of us still being alive, the girl and the old man. That ain't like Coburn to let people live after he has taken their cattle."

"He didn't have any choice," Ki said. "The girl had a pistol and she shot him in the arm."

"Shot him!" Pablo exclaimed.

"That's right. But she just winged him. He was rattled, though. That's why he took off."

Pablo chuckled. "Well, I'll be damned! The girl shot him! How about that!" he said with wonder. "Ain't she somethin' though?"

"She is," Ki said, turning to watch as Alice gently calmed her grandfather down.

"When will we be leavin'?" Pablo asked.

"Soon," Ki replied. "Let's go over and feed those horses, then saddle them. I think with any luck we should be back in Brownsville by early tomorrow morning."

There was a long pause, and then Pablo said, "Do you really think Miss Jessica can come up with a way to get that herd back?"

"Yes," Ki said simply.

"We'll see," Pablo said, doubt heavy in his voice. "I ain't sure she understands what she has stacked up against her."

"Don't worry, it will work out."

Pablo wasn't really listening. His eyes had a far, far away look, as he studied the receding dust. "All I want is a piece of John Coburn," he said. "I'm gonna kill that man or die trying."

"That's up to you," Ki said, "but we want these cattle and repayment for the herd that Miss Starbuck lost. That, and equal justice for all the dead cowboys."

"So," Pablo mused, "either way John Coburn dies."

Ki thought about it a minute and then he nodded his head. "That's right. Either way, with a gun or with a rope, he's going to die."

A wide smile slowly spread across Pablo's face. "I'm glad

we understand each other, samurai. Real glad! The last thing I want to do is to have to kill you, too."

Ki's eyes jerked up to the old man. He thought at first that Pablo was just fooling, but he could see the man was not. Pablo was dead serious. Ki knew that the old man would not try to harm him unless he stood in the way of vengeance, and if that happened, Ki knew that he could not trust Pablo Smith under any circumstances.

Instead of saying anything, Ki turned on his heel and moved over toward the corral. There were five horses, so they'd have one extra. He didn't exactly know which were the better saddle horses, but as he moved toward the barn, his thoughts concerned Jessica Starbuck—what she would say and what kind of plan she could possibly come up with to capture Coburn and the stolen herd.

Better, he thought as he grabbed his saddle, bridle, and harness and moved outside the tack room, better not to even worry about it. That was Jessie's business. His business was to protect her and to fight at her side. Jessie was the one who called the shots and made the decisions, though she often sought his opinion. If she did that, well and good, but if not, Ki would do exactly as she wished, because that was the samurai's way.

Chapter 10

When the knock sounded on her door, Jessie jumped from the chair where she had been reading. "Who is it?"

"It's Ki."

With a sigh of relief, Jessie hurried to the door and unlocked it. Ki pushed in first, and behind him came Pablo Smith, then a young woman, and finally an old man who looked pinched and crotchety.

"Jessie," Ki said once they were all inside and the door was closed, "allow me to make the introductions. This is Mrs. Alice Gruber and her grandfather, Buck Williams."

Jessie nodded. She had no idea what these two were doing here, but she was sure that Ki would tell her in a moment. And he did.

"I brought them back here," he concluded, "because I knew that you'd want them to join forces with us so that we could all ride against Coburn and his bloodthirsty rustlers."

Jessie nodded. "That's right," she said, looking to both the pretty young woman and her grandfather. "Mrs. Gruber, may I ask where your husband is?"

"He was shot," Alice said, "killed in a poker game just six months ago."

"I'm sorry to hear that."

"He was a gambler," the old man snapped in anger. "He wasn't worth a damn. He spent every dime he could get his hands on. He didn't care if his wife starved or—"

"Hush, Grandpa!" Alice said quickly, her face reddening with embarrassment. "There is no need to say those things anymore."

The old man looked away quickly, and in that one look Jessie could read everything in his mind. Alice Gruber's husband apparently hadn't been worth much, and her grandfather hated him even to his grave.

"We'll try to get your cattle back," Jessie said.

"How are you going to do that with just the five of us!" Buck Williams demanded.

"I'm going to hire some men. I've thought about it a lot. We can't use the law, because Texas justice stops at the border. That leaves me only the option of hiring gunmen."

"There are no good men in Brownsville," Buck warned. "Just a bunch of murdering cutthroats. Jackals and hounds is all there are."

"Perhaps," Jessie said, "but that's the kind of men we'll need in order to stomp out John Coburn and recapture your herd."

They all nodded, and Jessie said, "I'll start passing the word around. I'll pay a hundred dollars a man in advance and a hundred dollars when the job is done and we've recaptured the herd."

Pablo snorted, "Ain't no one going to go up against John Coburn and his men for two hundred dollars."

"Then I'll raise the ante even higher," Jessie said with determination. "I'll raise it just as high as need be in order to get a small group of tough men willing to fight on our side."

Pablo stared into Jessie's eyes, and when she did not turn her gaze away, he finally nodded with agreement. "For enough money," he said quietly, "men'll do any damn thing. Even ride south of the border into the jaws of death."

The very next day Jessie went to the local newspaper office, where she had fifty posters printed. The posters were very simple and stated only that a few good, brave men were needed for a dangerous job and that the pay would be very high. Interviews were to be taken the following afternoon in the town plaza.

Ki and Pablo also did their part. Throughout the day and into the evening they moved through the saloons, watching men, handing out the flyers, and answering questions. There was no sense in trying to fool anyone, and they readily admitted that this small force would be going into Mexico on a dangerous mission. They did not, however, state that it would be against John Coburn and his gang.

So it was the next afternoon, at the plaza, that Jessie found herself in the center of a large collection of hard-looking men, all packing guns and knives.

When Jessie stepped into their midst, there were hoots and whistles which abruptly died when the applicants realized that Jessie was the one who had advertised for gunfighters. Jessie stood up in the bed of a buckboard and studied the rough, motley gang.

One of them, horribly pocked across both cheeks, shouted up at her, "What the hell you doin' up there, lady? We're fightin' men."

"I understand that," Jessie said, "and that's what I'm looking for."

"You the one who's payin'?" the burly, scarred man shouted.

"That's right, and you'll be riding for me."

"The hell with that," the man shouted. "I ain't ridin' for no woman! Even one as good lookin' as you are!"

This caused an outburst of laughter, but Jessie's face remained dead serious. Just below her stood Ki, Pablo, and Buck. Alice had elected to remain in the hotel.

Jessie studied the big man. "My name is Jessica Starbuck and I'm the owner of the Circle Star Ranch. Perhaps some of you men have heard of it."

The men dipped their chins. The Circle Star Ranch was famous all over Texas, but one of the men shouted, "Hell, ma'am, you better go back home. What are you doin' down here in Satan's backyard?"

"I'm seeking justice," Jessie replied. "We need help and I'll pay very well for it. The men we choose must be top-notch gunfighters, and men not afraid to get into a real war. And when there is one, they must be willing to stand and fight to the death."

"Die!" shouted another man. "Woman, there ain't enough money in all of Texas to die for."

"Then you'd better leave," Jessie said, looking hard at the man, "because I can't guarantee the men I pick will all come back alive."

"Who the hell are we goin' after?" the burly man with the scarred cheeks asked.

Jessie was afraid that if she told them the truth, they'd all walk away. "Let's just say that we're going after men willing to fight."

"How much you payin'?"

Jessie paused for a moment. She knew this was the critical question and would decide if she got help or did not. "I'll pay one hundred when we go and another hundred when we come back with the herd."

"A herd?"

93

"That's right," Jessie said. "Mr. Buck Williams here," Jessie looked down at the old man, "had his herd stolen. We're going to recapture it and bring it back here to Brownsville."

The men in the crowd were silent for a minute, and then one of them said, "Could be you're talkin' about goin' up against John Coburn, ma'am?"

"Yes," Jessie said, after a moment's hesitation. "He's the one that stole the herd. He also stole my Circle Star herd and killed all my men as well as Mr. Williams's men. He's got to be stopped."

The men in the crowd exchanged glances. Suddenly, as if some unspoken word had passed between them, they turned and began to leave.

"Wait!" Jessie shouted. "I'll raise it another hundred dollars coming and going if you'll fight with us. That'll be four hundred dollars for every man that comes back alive."

One of them turned. "Ma'am," he said, "four hundred is more money than I could make in ten years in Brownsville. I'll ride with you."

"You will if you qualify," Jessie said. "We'll be interviewing each man and seeing how he handles a gun."

"That suits me just right down to the ground," the man said with a quick nod of agreement.

"Good!" Jessie looked at the others. "Are there any others willing to fight for four hundred dollars, cash?"

Again the men exchanged glances and this time most stayed. A few, however, lowered their heads and walked away. When there were about twenty tough gunmen remaining, Jessie folded her arms across her ample bosom.

"All right," she said, "we'll start off with a little target practice. Follow me."

They marched up the street, causing store owners and passersby to gawk with curiosity. Jessie paid them no attention. When she finally reached the edge of town, she stopped and told the men to form a rough line. They didn't like it. They weren't used to taking orders, but they lined up. Jessie took the first man, the heavyset one with the scars on his cheeks. He was a fierce-looking individual, built like a tree trunk, very powerful, very savage-looking.

"What's your name?" Jessie asked.

"Tom," the man rumbled.

"Well, Tom, you see that old rusty bean can out there?"

He followed her gaze. "Yeah, I see it."

"Let's see what you can do with it."

"From here?" Tom asked. "Why, ma'am, that's more than fifty yards and it ain't much of a can."

"If you can't hit it, Tom, I can't use you."

"I'll hit it," Tom said. With that he reached down and yanked out his gun, raised it for a second, aimed, and began to fire. The first shot missed, but the second slug hit the can and sent it flying. It landed, and Tom drilled it again and again, missed the fourth time, and shot it twice more.

"You're on," Jessie said, pleased by the show of marksmanship.

Tom nodded his head with the slightest of grins. "Ma'am, if all these men are goin' to be shootin' at cans, you're goin' to need some more of 'em."

"That's right," Jessie said. "Why don't you go gather up a few and we'll see what we can do? I'd appreciate it very much."

She smiled at Tom and he smiled back. It was a mean, ornery-looking smile, but somehow, underneath all that ugliness and those scars, Jessie detected a pretty good man. Tom would fight, she was sure of that much, and she hoped that most of these others she was about to test would share the same kind of grit and toughness.

95

For the next two hours the remaining men stepped forward and demonstrated their gun skills. Some were clearly incompetent and missed badly. Toward the end two of them just walked away, knowing that they could not even begin to pass Jessie's rigorous test. When it was all said and done, Jessie had an even dozen real gunmen. They were a sorry collection, filthy, down at the heels, and looking more like they should be in prison than running free, but she knew that each one of them was capable of putting up a hard fight.

"All right," she said to the twelve, "we'll be leaving in about two hours."

"Two hours!" Tom snorted. "My God, woman, what's the hurry?"

"The hurry," Jessie said, "is that Buck Williams's herd has been stolen and we understand Coburn will waste no time delivering them to the Gulf and then selling them to a buccaneer named Lafitte."

"You got that right," Tom said, "but still and all, ma'am, we're gonna need a little time to blow off some steam before we go. You know . . . Besides, we got some money comin'."

"You'll get your money," Jessie said, "when we ride out."

"Now, ma'am," Tom argued. "I want my half the money right now and—"

Jessie nailed him with her eyes. "You'll take the money when we leave, or you can step out of this, Tom. I'm calling the shots from now on."

The rough man tried to stare her down and break her will, but when Jessie's gaze matched and held his own, he finally weakened and snorted, "Goddammit! A man deserves to blow off a little steam before he's goin' to ride across the Rio Grande against the likes of John Coburn. It's the least you could do, ma'am."

"I'm sorry," Jessie said. "I need each and every one of you and I need you sober and clear-thinking. You can celebrate when you've been paid off." Jessie looked at all of the men. "And in case any of you are thinking that perhaps you can ride out the first night with the money I've already given you, forget about it. We'd track you down, no matter how far you ran, and kill you."

The men stared and believed her. Jessie paused for a moment and then said, "And by the way, just so you know that even though I'm a woman, I'm plenty capable in a gunfight, I want to show you something."

With that Jessie reached down and drew the gun from her shapely hip. It came up swiftly, not as swiftly as a professional gunfighter's, but very fast. The gun bucked in her hand six times, so rapidly it sounded like one single roar, and the tin can before her was jerked from side to side in the air. It was a remarkable display of shooting, the best they had seen all afternoon. The men stared in amazement. When the can dropped, Jessie's gun hammer clicked down on an empty cartridge. She holstered the gun.

"There," she said. "That ought to show you that I intend to fight beside you."

Tom whistled softly. "Ma'am, you can do anything you damn sure want right beside me."

Jessie allowed herself a half smile. "Thanks," she said. "But fighting is all I have in mind."

There were several snickers, but Jessie ignored them. Then, with Ki and Buck Williams at her side, she turned and started to walk away. "We'll meet right here at this spot in two hours. Be ready to ride. Have enough provisions for three days."

"Three days, huh?" someone said. "Maybe that's about all the time we have left to live."

Jessie turned back to see which man had spoken, but there was no way of knowing. "I'm not guaranteeing you anything," she said to the men she'd just hired, "except a lot

of money for those of you who survive. But consider this—
you could be killed down here over something as trivial as a
glass of whiskey. I'm offering you a chance to make a fresh
start. With four hundred dollars, you'll be able to buy a small
herd of cattle, a share in a profitable mine, or even a small
business."

"I want to go to California," one of the men said. "Want
to see if there's any gold left. If there ain't I'll go to the
Comstock. I heard they got pretty women there and lots of
silver yet to be dug."

"You heard right," Jessie said, "and you'll have plenty of
money to get a good start."

"That's enough for me," the man said. "I'm in all the way."

"Good." Jessie studied their tough faces one by one.
"We're all in this together. We're either going to win or
we're going to die."

The men nodded with understanding, and then they went
to make their preparations for the ride into Mexico.

When they returned to their hotel room, Alice was eager to
know what had happened. When Jessie explained that she
had found a dozen good, hard fighters that would accompany
them down into Mexico, Alice looked a little pale, but nodded with satisfaction.

"I'm glad to hear that," she said. "Our cowboys were all
good men. They didn't deserve to die, and everything my
grandfather and I own is in that herd of cattle."

"I know that," Jessie said. "I lost a herd twice that size,
but I've got a lot more cattle back at Circle Star. This is
your entire stake. I mean to see that we recapture it before
your herd is loaded on the ships and sent down to Central
America."

"Do you think we have a chance?" Alice asked suddenly.

"We always have a chance," Jessie answered. "Hopefully, what we have is the element of surprise. If we can catch John Coburn and his gang off-guard with your cattle, I think we'll do very well against them. But if we don't at least have the element of surprise, we're probably going to lose."

She hesitated a moment, looking into the young widow's eyes. "Alice, you don't have to go. In fact, I think it would be better if you stayed here."

"No," Alice said. "I'm coming. I couldn't live with myself if I didn't come. That's my herd as well as Grandpa's. It's all we've got."

"All right," Jessie said. "Can you handle a gun?"

"I can't hit the side of a bar with a pistol," Alice replied, "but I'm a little better with a rifle."

"What about a shotgun?" Jessie asked. "Would you be able to fire a shotgun?"

Alice nodded. "Grandpa has an old double-barreled shotgun loaded with bird shot. I've shot plenty of quail, grouse, and pheasant."

"Then we'll find you a double-barreled shotgun, only we won't load it with bird shot. We'll load it with something substantially heavier."

"All right," Alice said quietly. "And don't worry, when it comes time to fight, I won't run."

"I know you won't," Jessie said. "None of us will. It's going to be a fight to the death."

They looked into each other's eyes and Alice turned away. Jessie glanced sideways at the samurai and saw him watching the girl closely. She wondered what was on the samurai's mind. Most often, like now, he was totally inscrutable, keeping his thoughts buried deep behind a mask. Did he think she was crazy to be taking those rough men down into Mexico? Jessie hoped not. And, as she rarely did, she felt a little doubt. But she pushed it aside, and hurriedly began to make her own preparations. There was much to be done—supplies to be bought, horses to be readied and saddled, ammunition and weapons to be checked.

"We haven't much time," she said. "Let's get busy."

★

Chapter 11

Late that afternoon, they splashed across the Rio Grande and circled Matamoros, heading south. Ki, of course, knew exactly where Coburn's hacienda was, and so they moved steadily across the arid country. At last they came to the hills that surrounded the valley where the rustlers' ranch lay hidden.

"It's just beyond those hills," Ki said.

Jessie replied, "Why don't you and I go up there to the crest of that hill and take a look? The rest of you wait here."

Jessie and Ki galloped their horses forward, and when they neared the crest of the hill, they dismounted, tied their horses to a brush, and traveled the rest of the way on foot. They crawled the last few yards, until they had a clear view of the valley below.

"There they are," Ki said.

A moment later Buck Williams and Alice were at their side. "We couldn't stay behind," Alice explained. "We had to see if they had our cattle or not."

"Is that them?" Jessie asked, pointing down at the small herd grazing peacefully below.

"That's our herd," Buck Williams said. "No doubt about it, Miss Starbuck."

"We'll do our best to get them back," Jessie said.

"When do we start?" Alice asked.

She thought about it a moment and said, "Why wait? Let's strike tonight. They won't be expecting us and there is a possibility that they might leave early in the morning and we would lose our element of surprise."

"Suits me," Buck said.

Ki approved of the plan.

They moved away from the hillside and slowly walked on back down to meet the collection of Brownsville gunfighters.

"Well?" Tom demanded.

"They're there," Jessie said. "The herd, Coburn's rustlers, all of them."

"So what are we going to do now?"

"We're going to attack."

"Right now?"

"No," Jessie said. "We'll wait until midnight."

"Be better," Tom said, "if we waited till a couple hours before daybreak."

Jessie pursed her lips. "All right," she said, "that probably would be better. We'll come in from the north and the south. No one opens fire until we are on top of them, or a sentry has sounded the alarm. Then we stampede the herd back in this direction and make sure Coburn and his men never raid into Texas again."

"I think," Ki said, "it is important to capture their horses."

"The hell with their horses," Tom argued. "We either finish off John Coburn now, kill him and every last one 'em, or they'll get more horses and come across the border after us. There'll be no end to it if Coburn lives, Miss Starbuck. I don't want to spend the rest of my life lookin' over my shoulder."

102

Jessie grimly nodded. "I agree," she said. "Unless they throw down their guns in surrender, we'll take no prisoners."

The dozen men nodded in stony silence. Without any conversation, they made camp and settled down to wait until early the next morning. Everyone was grim-faced and on edge.

Jessie said, "I'll post guards and the rest of us can eat cold jerky or whatever we've got in our saddlebags, then sleep as much as we can until it's time to fight."

Jessie found it impossible to fall asleep that night and was still awake at midnight. As she'd expected, the samurai had taken a lookout position by the crest of the hill overlooking the rustlers' valley. He watched the dark forms of the cattle grazing in the moonlight. His mind was on the battle that would soon begin, and he did not even see Alice as she moved up the hill to kneel down beside him.

"Are you afraid?" she asked.

Ki looked sideways at her. "No."

"I don't understand that," Alice said. "I'm so frightened my palms are sweating."

Ki took her hands in his own. Her palms were damp. "Maybe you should stay with our horses."

"No!" She shook her head violently. "I have as much at stake here as anyone."

"All right." Ki turned to gaze back down at the peaceful valley below. It was hard to believe that, in just a few hours, men would be fighting and dying.

Alice said, "Have you known Miss Starbuck long?"

"Yes," Ki answered. "We've been friends a long time."

"Do you work for her?"

"I do," Ki replied.

"Are you . . ." Alice's words trailed off.

"Am I what?" Ki asked.

"Are you in love with her?"

103

Ki smiled. "In a way," he admitted, "though we've never been lovers."

"I don't understand that."

"It's difficult to explain." Ki frowned. "You see, I am a samurai. A samurai's code is to serve his master."

"Master?" Alice asked. "You're not a slave."

"No," Ki conceded, "I'm not a slave, but the samurai's way of life is the life that I choose. It gives me purpose."

Alice stretched out on the grass and placed her hands behind her head. "You mean you can't have purpose without serving someone as if they were your master?"

Ki chuckled. "It would take me hours and hours to explain it to you, Alice. And even then you would never really understand."

"Maybe someday we'll have hours and hours," Alice said, "if we live through this night." She reached out and touched his arm. "I've been watching you," she said. "You seem so relaxed and confident."

Ki shrugged. "I've been in many battles, I've trained myself to fight as a samurai. I'm not afraid."

"I think the other men are," Alice said. "I can just feel the tension down there."

"It's not fear," Ki said. "Those are hard men. They know that life is worth very little on the border and that this is a chance for them to make a lot of money. The best chance they may ever have, short of robbing a stage or a bank."

"Yes, you're right," Alice said. "Would you . . ." She could not finish her request and turned away.

"Would I what?" Ki asked, pulling her back around to face him.

"Would you hold me?"

Without a word Ki reached out and took her into his arms. Alice felt warm, but he also felt her tremble. She snuggled up close to him and raised her face. When she closed her

104

eyes, Ki kissed her. He felt her shiver and grip him harder. She whispered in his ear.

"Please make love to me."

Ki raised his head. "Here? Now?"

"Yes!"

Ki was surprised but recovered quickly. Slowly he unbuttoned her blouse and then helped remove the rest of her clothes. When Ki mounted her, she clung to him as if he were her salvation, and when he gazed down at her face, he saw tears.

"What's wrong, Alice? Am I hurting you?"

"No, I'm crying because of my late husband," she said. "He wasn't much of a man. He was selfish. He was mean-spirited. He drank and gambled too much, but when he made love to me like this, it was—"

"Hush," Ki said, covering her lips as his body moved on hers. "You don't have to explain anything."

Alice held him tightly as he worked over her slowly, then faster and faster. When she cried out with pleasure, he softly muffled her lips with his mouth, as his own body stiffened with release and he filled her with his seed.

A few minutes later, as he tried to roll off of her, she clung to him with desperation. "No, please, just stay like this for a few more minutes."

Ki remained motionless. Stars twinkled overhead. Coyotes howled off in the distance, and down below in the valley cattle grazed quietly in the semidarkness. It was much later when Ki lifted from her and dressed.

Alice avoided looking at him, and when Ki touched her face, he said, "What's the matter?"

"I feel a little ashamed."

"Ashamed?"

"Yes. I was so wanton just now. I don't know what got into me."

"You were afraid. You needed to be held and loved. Sometimes we all need someone. There is nothing wrong with that."

"But I'm a married woman!"

"You're a widow. You had a husband and he's dead. There's nothing to be ashamed about."

Alice kissed Ki softly. "Isn't it about time that we should get our horses and guns ready?"

"Yes," Ki said.

He took her hand, and together they walked down the hillside, toward Jessie and the men, who waited below.

★

Chapter 12

Jessica could tell by the alignment of the stars when it was about four o'clock in the morning. In another hour the sun would leave a faint gray mark on the eastern horizon, which would gradually lighten and then turn a brilliant crimson and gold. She and her men rode over the crest of the hill, then down into the valley through the stolen herd of cattle.

"All right," Jessie whispered as they drew nearer the hacienda. "Spread out!"

As they fanned out across the yard, all was quiet until a dog began to bark furiously. A moment later Jessie heard muffled shouts from within the hacienda and saw the flash of gunfire. Her men, rather than retreat and be caught out in the open come daylight, knew they had no choice but to charge. Two died instantly, but the others were able to reach the yard, dismount, and take cover behind the outlying buildings.

Ki was right beside Jessie, and he said, "I was hoping we would be able to get a little closer before that dog caught wind of us."

"Speaking of which, here it comes!" Jessie exclaimed as the dog came streaking across the yard, hurtling toward them.

It was coming right at Jessie, and it would have launched itself at her throat if the samurai hadn't blocked its path of attack. He caught it by the scruff of the neck, and even though the fierce animal must have weighed a hundred pounds, the samurai flipped it completely upside down and slammed it down on the ground. It yelped, and then, as it tried to bite his wrist, Ki's right hand lifted, slashed downward, and struck the animal's neck. Jessie heard bone snap, and the vicious animal emitted a death rattle.

The gun battle was raging. Jessie yelled for her men to try and circle the hacienda.

"The front window," Ki said, pointing. "I haven't seen a gun flash there yet. I'm going through it."

"No!" Jessie protested, grabbing at his arm.

But the samurai was already moving. In his black *ninja* outfit, even Jessie could barely see him in the strong moonlight. Ki stayed low to the ground and seemed to fly effortlessly until he was underneath the window.

"My heavens, he'll be killed for sure!" Alice cried.

"No, he won't," Jessie said.

When one of the rustlers poked his gun through a window, Jessie fired instinctively and had the satisfaction of hearing the man scream as his gun shot a flame skyward.

"Got him!"

Once inside the hacienda, the samurai hurried through a dark bedroom to reach the hallway. The moment he opened the door, the sound of heavy gunfire filled his ears and the air inside the hacienda was thick with gunsmoke. The samurai slipped outside, into the hallway, and moved cautiously forward. When he came to the end of the hall, he saw through the smoke and poor light the immense silhouette of Coburn and others of his gang as the battle raged. Ki deduced that there had been five outlaws besides Coburn himself, and he could see at least three dead men on the tile floor. Maybe there were others somewhere in the hacienda, but Ki had the feeling this was all that had survived the first attack.

Ki flattened to the ground and began to slink forward. Suddenly an outlaw screamed and back-pedaled across the room. He crashed over a table and landed, kicking in death, just a few feet from where Ki had stopped, frozen and waiting.

"Son of a bitch!" another outlaw screamed. "They're gonna wipe us out!"

"Shut up!" Coburn bellowed. "Shut up and just keep firing!"

"But who the hell are they! Is it the Texas Rangers come across the border after us?"

"I said shut up!" Coburn yelled. "It doesn't matter who they are. They're out to get us. We either kill them or they kill us."

"But we're surrounded," the man cried, rising panic in his voice. "I say we ought to surrender before they kill us all!"

Ki watched Coburn lift his gun and point it directly at the beaten man. "One more word from you, Dean, and I'll put a bullet through your head myself. Now get over to the window and keep firing!"

Dean did as he was told.

Ki waited a few more seconds, trying to decide what to do next. He could hear shouts off in another room and then a man burst into view. "John, they're almost to the back door! We can't hold 'em off any longer. I'm all that's left. What are we going to do!"

"Dean, get back there!"

Dean took off, and a second later, Ki heard the sounds of a fierce gun battle raging from the back of the hacienda. He thought he heard a man scream in death.

Now Ki saw there were only two outlaws left in the room besides John Coburn. The samurai leaped at the nearest man, who was so intent on firing his gun that he did not even see the samurai until it was too late. Ki's hand arced downward and struck the man at the base of his neck, and the outlaw slumped to the floor. An instant later Ki leaped upon the back of another man, driving his *tanto* blade into his body even as his hand muffled the sound of the last cry the man would ever utter. Twice more he plunged his knife into the outlaw's body, and when the man was still, Ki twisted away and stood up, just in time to see Coburn swing around.

"Ed, what . . ." Coburn roared in hatred and opened fire with the smoking six-gun clenched in his massive fist.

Ki felt the burn of a bullet striking his shoulder. He felt himself spin halfway around, and then Coburn cursed and fired again. The samurai dropped and rolled, knowing he was going to die unless he could find cover. But the giant pounced on him, grabbed his hair, and tried to break Ki's neck. Ki twisted onto his back and kicked the giant in the belly. Coburn grunted but did not move. "I'm going to break you in half with my own hands," he shouted. "I should have killed you long before now."

He raised his gun, but at that instant Ki threw him off balance, and the outlaw leader's gun belched a bullet into the tile floor. Coburn fell heavily, the wind exploding from his lungs, and Ki leaped on top of him. Then they were tearing at each other, slashing and gouging, punching as hard as they could, each seeking a vital organ to rupture. They rolled over and over, and Ki knew that he was at a great disadvantage. Not only was Coburn stronger, but he was much heavier.

Ki could feel his strength fade because of his shoulder wound. He had lost his knife, but now he managed to slip his hand inside his tunic, desperately fumbling for a *shuriken*

110

star blade. He located one and dragged it out. Coburn was pounding at his face. Ki felt himself losing consciousness. With the last of his reserves, he reached back with his right hand and drove the star blade upward.

"Ahhhhh!" Coburn screamed, his hands clutching at the star blade buried between his eyes.

Ki used that moment to grab Coburn by the shirtfront and throw him sideways. The giant was screaming, blood filling his eyes. Blindly he began to slash at Ki with his now empty six-gun. Ki took a glancing blow to the side of the head and momentarily lost consciousness. When he awoke a few seconds later, Coburn's hand had found his throat. Ki kicked and struggled like a rabbit caught in a noose. Even with the star blade buried in his face, John Coburn was inhumanly strong. Ki kicked up with his heels and managed to hook them around the giant's neck. With all his strength Ki pulled Coburn over backward.

Coburn was probably dying, because the star blade was buried deeply in his forehead. Yet, he wasn't through fighting. He struck and clawed until Ki realized he was still in the fight of his life. Again they rolled over twice. The samurai managed to reach into his tunic and grab another star blade. Clutching it in his fist, Ki slashed blindly at the giant.

The star blade penetrated Coburn's throat. Blood poured over the samurai and he heard Coburn's death rattle. Finally, Coburn toppled over sideways. His boot heels thumped against the tile floor for several seconds, and one useless arm beat up and down. The man's head rolled back and forth, and Ki was glad for the semidarkness as he crawled away, gasping for air. A moment later the sounds of Coburn's dying finally ended.

The samurai struggled for air, wondering if his throat were broken. It took him several long, agonizing moments before

111

he was able to breathe properly, and when he could, he wobbled to his feet, hand reaching toward the bullet hole in his shoulder.

He cried, "Jessie, Coburn is dead. His men are almost through. Come on!"

Jessie heard the samurai just as she and her Brownsville gunfighters killed the last of the outlaw band, except for one man, who threw down his gun and begged for mercy. Kerosene lanterns were lit and Jessie rushed to the samurai's side. "My God!" she exclaimed in shock at all the blood covering him. "Are you dying?"

"No," Ki said. "It's not my blood. It's Coburn's."

"Thank God!" Jessie cried. "Where are you hurt?"

"The shoulder."

Jessie tore the samurai's tunic off. A quick glance told her the bullet wound was not fatal, and yet it was quite serious. The samurai was losing far too much blood. Very quickly she tore strips from his tunic, and when Alice arrived with her grandfather, she helped Jessie bandage the wound.

"Is he going to live?" Alice asked tearfully.

"You bet I am," Ki said. "I'm going to be just fine, so you can stop worrying and go count your cattle."

"To hell with them right now," Alice swore. "Your life is worth more than the whole herd."

"Not to me it ain't," Buck Williams growled.

Jessie studied the wound closer. "Ki, we'll have to get you to a doctor," she said. "There's still a bullet in your shoulder."

Ki had already guessed that much. "Jessie, I would prefer you remove it rather than a doctor from Matamoros or Brownsville."

"All right. As soon as I check on all the others, I'll do my best."

A quick check revealed that five of Jessie's men were dead, leaving seven alive, two of them seriously wounded

112

and one with only a bullet graze across the forehead. The lone captured outlaw was bound and thrown into a corner. Jessie came back to the samurai.

"I'll need hot water and your *tanto* blade."

"I lost it somewhere in the darkness."

"Here it is!" Alice said, spotting the long, thin knife, which was as sharp as any razor.

When Alice brought hot water back to the room a short time later, Jessie cleaned the samurai's wounded shoulder.

"I'm afraid this is worse than I first thought," she told him. "I suspect the bullet is deep inside."

"You can get the slug out," Ki said. "You've done it before."

"Yes," Jessie said, "I have, but . . ."

"Don't think about it," Ki gritted. "Just do it."

Jessie nodded. She called for the hot water again, and with her hired gunmen holding kerosene lamps overhead and the first rays of the sun firing the eastern horizon, she bent to her task.

She had removed many bullets before and prayed this one would be easy. Sometimes it was more expedient to roll the patient over and see if the bullet was closer to the exit than the entry. But in this case, Jessie worried that the bullet might have struck some bone.

"I might have to probe very deep," she said to the samurai. "Would you like some whiskey?"

"I'll be fine," Ki said. "Just get the bullet out."

Jessie nodded. She looked at Tom, then to Alice, and finally to old Buck Williams. Taking a calming breath, she cut a deep incision.

The samurai barely flinched, though Alice's hand flew to her mouth and she looked away quickly. Jessie focused all of her concentration on the wound. She made a second incision, forming an X, and then she peeled back the flesh

113

and slipped the blade deep down inside. She closed her eyes and probed with the blade. When it struck bone, she gently edged it deeper into the shoulder.

Finally, she felt what she had been searching for all along, and that was metal touching metal.

"I think I found it," Jessie said, "but it's very deep." Sweat was popping out all over her body as she slowly began to work the lead slug out of the samurai's shoulder. It took almost ten minutes, and the blood flowed so freely that she was afraid Ki might die of blood loss before she was able to get the bullet out and the wound closed.

Finally, however, she was able to pull the slug out. It was misshapen and evil-looking, with a splinter of bone wedged in between some of the twisted metal.

"Ki, can you hear me?"

The samurai was still conscious. He was breathing steadily, deeply.

"We've got it out, now," Jessie said. "At least all this bleeding will cleanse the wound. I'm going to apply a hot compress to draw out the last of the poison before I bandage."

Ki said nothing. He did not even feel the scalding compress that Jessie laid on the wound. In a few moments he drifted into a deep sleep as Jessie expertly bandaged the shoulder.

Tom and the Brownsville gunfighters who had not been killed in the fight drifted quietly outside to smoke and talk of the hard battle they'd just won.

Jessie looked up at her friends. "If Ki doesn't die of blood loss," she said, "he'll be just fine."

Alice was very pale.

As the sun rose, they could see it burning through the easternmost window of the hacienda, casting light upon dead bodies and the carnage of their gutsy predawn assault.

"So many dead," Alice said.

"These are the same men," Jessie reminded her, "that gunned down your poor cowboys without any compassion whatsoever. They would also have killed you and your grandfather given the opportunity."

"Or worse," Buck Williams said, looking at his granddaughter. "They'd have probably done worse."

"What else can we do for Ki?" Alice asked, her fingers shaking as she caressed the samurai's cheek.

"Nothing except to let him sleep," Jessie said. "One thing for certain, we cannot move Ki until the wound clots."

"And then?"

"We can make that decision when we get to it," Jessie said, climbing stiffly to her feet. She took a final look at Ki and then walked out into the yard. There were bodies lying about, both her men and the rustlers. She walked through them to the edge of the ranch yard, to face the rising sun. There were clouds on the eastern horizon, and the sun gilded them as the sky gradually turned from pink to russet to a pale, soft blue. It was going to be a beautiful day, Jessie thought, and it was too bad that anyone had to die at all.

Why is there so much killing in this world, she wondered. Why so much greed and hatred, so much senseless taking of lives? Jessie shook her head. She didn't know the answers to any of those questions. She only knew that men would always fight to the death for what they wanted, be it a crust of bread among the poorest, or a crown among the most high. There would never be equality in this world; Jessie knew that. As long as some men had much more than others, there would always be hatred and jealousy and killing.

Jessie breathed deeply the clear morning air. She was sure that Ki would be all right and that he would recover remarkably soon from his wound because of his amazing recuperative powers. What they needed to do now, she thought, was

115

to figure out how they might also snare the buccaneers that John Coburn had worked with so well and so long. It seemed to Jessie that if she did not stop Luke Lafitte, other men would soon take Coburn's place stealing and raiding along the border.

Even as she thought this and watched the sun detach itself from the earth, Jessie formed a plan. She would take this herd on down to the Gulf to use it as a lure in order to trap Luke Lafitte. She took a deep breath. That's what needed to be done, although she wasn't sure she could talk Buck Williams and Alice into allowing her to do it. Jessie would, of course, offer to buy their herd; if it were lost again, she would reimburse them at top dollar.

It all depended, Jessie decided, on whether they believed and trusted her. But never mind that for now, Jessie thought as she knuckled her eyes. What she and her men needed was sleep. Tomorrow they would evaluate Ki's condition, and Jessie fully expected that the samurai would be alert and ready to help implement her plan against Lafitte.

Off in the distance she saw a coyote trotting across the barren hilltop near where she and her men had camped the night before. Perhaps the coyote had found a scrap of meat or some other leftover for breakfast. It looked small and thin. The coyote sensed her watchful green eyes and froze for a minute to watch her. Across the distance their eyes seemed to lock, but their minds could not possibly meet. "Your life isn't any easier than mine, is it?" Jessie murmured. In answer the coyote sat, raised his head, and howled at the rising sun.

For some reason this cheered Jessie. She took it as a good omen. She smiled, lifted her shoulders, and then returned to the hacienda. They would clean it out, and then she would find a bedroom and catch up on her sleep. She would keep constant watch on Ki, of course, and be sure that he was healing well and that there was no more bleeding. And there were other wounded besides him that needed her attention.

Give things time to heal, she thought. She would need to post a few of her survivors out to guard the herd and the lone outlaw they had taken prisoner.

What would she do with him? Jessie wondered. Could he help her some way? She had barely glanced at the man, a thin, lanky sort, with a drooping handlebar mustache and shifty eyes. Certainly he was not the kind of man to be trusted, and yet, if she paid him, he might provide her with some useful information.

★

Chapter 13

Jessie was content to remain in the hacienda for two weeks. By the end of that time, Ki was moving well and Jessie's men were in good spirits, although they were starting to get restless to return to Brownsville and spend the money Jessie had promised to have wired from her main bank in Santa Fe.

When Jessie was sure that Ki was well on the mend, she knew it was time to interrogate their prisoner and perhaps speak of her plan to snare the buccaneers.

She said to the samurai, "I would like to speak to our captive."

Ki smiled. "I was wondering when we were going to stop lying around all day and get busy."

He left and soon returned with the captive, whose wrists were bound behind his back. The outlaw appeared haggard, and it was clear to Jessie that he was struggling to keep up a brave front.

"Untie his hands," Jessie ordered.

Ki untied the outlaw's hands.

"Sit down."

"I'll stand," the man said belligerently.

"Sit!" Ki said, grabbing him by the shirt and rudely pushing him into a chair, taking care not to reinjure his mending shoulder.

Jessie stood before the man, hands on hips. "Your life hangs in the balance, depending on what you tell us."

"I ain't tellin' you nothin'!"

"Don't be a fool. John Coburn is dead, which means only you can save your own life."

The outlaw started to say something and then clamped his jaw shut.

"Listen," Jessie said. "What I want to know is where I can find Luke Lafitte."

The prisoner blinked, indicating that Jessie had taken him by surprise.

"You are wondering why I want to see Luke Lafitte, aren't you?"

"Yeah."

"What is your name?"

There was a moment of pause before Ki grabbed the outlaw by the hair and jerked his head back.

"Doug Allen!" the man screamed. "Let go of me!"

Ki released the man's hair. He looked into Allen's face and said, "You must learn some better manners. You are speaking to Miss Jessica Starbuck."

"It's all right," Jessie said. "Doug, the reason I'm asking is simple. Luke Lafitte and men like him have been causing a lot of hardship all along this border for too long. I want to stop him."

"You can't stop Lafitte," Allen said. "Not with this handful of men."

"That's what they said in Brownsville about John Coburn's gang, yet look what we've done."

Allen's eyes tightened at the corners. "You got lucky. You caught us by surprise."

119

"We'll catch the buccaneers by surprise, too," Jessie promised. "What I need is a way to make contact."

"I don't know a thing."

Jessie looked at Ki. The samurai raised his hand to strike, and Allen's nerve suddenly broke.

"All right! All right! I'll help you."

"That's better," Jessie said quietly. "Now, tell me all you can about Luke Lafitte."

"What's to tell?"

"Tell me what he looks like. Tell me how old he is. Tell me what his habits are. Tell me what he likes and what he doesn't like. Tell me how he operates."

Allen frowned. "He's about . . . oh . . . thirty years old, I guess. Black hair, strong, and with a little saber scar down his left cheek. He's a showy sort of man and likes the ladies. But then, who don't?"

"How many men does he have in his band of buccaneers?"

"Twenty or thirty. Sometimes more."

"I see. And where does he stay?"

"About sixty miles south of here. That's where we were going to drive the cattle."

"Where they'd load the cattle on the buccaneer ships," Jessie said, "and send them down to Central America?"

"That's about the size of it. Ain't nothin' fancy. There's a dock. We drive the cattle onto the dock. It's like a big loading chute. Run 'em right onto the dock and funnel 'em right onto the ship. He's got another ship that he uses fer other things."

"Like what?" Jessie asked coldly.

"Things like slaves—whatever," Allen said noncommittally.

Jessie nodded. "So this town where the buccaneers' ships can be found, what's it like? How big is it?"

"It's smaller than Brownsville or Matamoros," Allen said. "Mostly all Mexicans, but there are some whites. In fact, quite a few. They don't work for anybody particular. When they are runnin' from a U.S. Marshal or a Texas Ranger, it's a good place to hide."

"I'll bet," Jessie said cryptically. "Do you know if Lafitte is in this town right now?"

"No. He's gone most of the time. No one would dare ask where he comes from or goes."

"What's the town's name?"

"San Miguel."

"Where does Lafitte stay in this town?"

Allen was so slow to answer that Ki grabbed him by one of his ears and pulled it hard.

"Ouch!" Allen cried. "All right, all right! Lafitte's got his own hacienda. It's at the south end of the town, overlooking the bay."

"Is it fortified?"

"Yes."

"And I suppose it has adobe walls."

"That's right," Allen snapped. "He's got guards, too."

"How many?" Ki asked.

"I don't know. Five, ten, all times, day and night. Both when he's there or gone. Makes no difference."

"Where do they hold cattle until they are loaded on their ships?"

"There are pens," Allen said. "Lots of pens."

"How does Lafitte pay for the cattle?"

Allen thought about it a moment. "I don't know," he said. "I never got paid. Mostly, though, I suspect he's got a vault on his property. All I know is he seems to have lots of money and he buys all the stolen cattle he can. Buys 'em cheap and probably sells 'em for twice as much in Central America."

"Okay," Jessie said, standing up. "You know Lafitte personally, don't you?"

There was a long silence. Ki kicked Allen in the ribs none

121

too gently. Allen grunted and Ki drew back his foot again.

Allen said, "Yeah, I know him!"

"Very good," Jessie said. "Then you'll make the introductions."

Allen paled a little. "He'll skewer me on his sword."

"He carries a sword?" Ki asked with surprise.

"That's right. A big sword. He wears a bandanna around his forehead. He looks just like you'd expect a buccaneer to look. He speaks at least four languages I know of, and he has the respect of his men. They say he is damn smart and he must be to have stayed alive this long. There are plenty of men who would like to have what Luke Lafitte's got."

"All right," Jessie said. "I'll have a talk with Buck Williams and Alice. If it's all right with them we'll drive the herd down to San Miguel."

Jessie called her friends together and said, "As you can see, Ki has almost completely mended. Now we need to make a decision."

Buck Williams frowned. "What decision? We are going to drive the herd back to our Texas ranch, aren't we?"

"That's one possibility," Jessie said, choosing her words carefully. "But there is an alternative."

"What are you talking about?" the old man demanded. "These are our cattle. You helped Alice and me get 'em back. We want to take 'em home!"

"Listen," Jessie said, speaking to the young woman and her grandfather. "I understand that you have worked hard and I understand that these cattle mean everything to you."

"They're all we've got," Alice said, "you know that."

"Yes, I do," Jessie said, "and I'll buy them from you if anything goes wrong, because I want to drive these cattle down to the port city of San Miguel and trap Luke Lafitte."

"What!" Buck Williams cried. "Lady, you must be out of your mind!"

"No," Jessie said, "at least I don't think I am. And your herd will be our lure."

"Now wait just a minute," Alice said.

"Listen," Jessie interrupted. "You know that I own the Circle Star Ranch and I'm good for whatever money I pledge to you. I'll buy this herd. In fact, I need a thousand cattle to deliver to Corpus Christi. It's too late now to meet the contract, but perhaps something can be salvaged through a good friend of mine in New Orleans. So, I'll buy your cattle here and now and I'll pay top dollar. What we're talking about, then, is whether or not you will sell me the herd on a promissory note."

Buck glanced sideways at his granddaughter. "I don't know," he said. "I never thought about selling 'em like this. I always demand cash in hand."

"Think about it," Jessie said. "I will give you top dollar, and if you write out a bill of sale, I'll write you out a voucher right now for the money. I'm good for it, I swear. In fact, I do have almost a thousand dollars cash that I can give you on account."

"A thousand dollars?"

"That's right," Jessie said.

Buck whistled. "Why, ma'am, that'd only be about half of what those cattle of ours are worth."

"That's right," Jessie said. "But I want you to understand very clearly that no matter what happens in San Miguel, you will be fully paid for your cattle. I guess what I'm asking is— will you help us?"

"Sure we will," Alice blurted. She looked at her grandfather and took his arm. "Grandpa?"

"Yeah," he said. "I'm thinkin' about our four dead cowboys. I'm thinkin' about all the other people I know who lost cattle and I'm thinkin' about if we don't stamp this thing out, it could happen to us again."

"That's right," Jessie said. "So, why don't we see if we can trap and finish off these ruthless buccaneers?"

"What are our chances?" Alice asked.

"We have about the same chance we had of killing the Coburn gang, and we succeeded rather handsomely, didn't we?"

"Yes," Alice said, "but maybe we were . . ."

"No," Jessie said, "we weren't just lucky."

"But we're fewer now," Alice argued. "We had a dozen hired guns. And Ki . . ."

"I'm almost back as good as new," the samurai told her. "And I will be by the time we get your herd to San Miguel."

"I know," Jessie said. "And as far as the others are concerned, I'll promise Tom and them even more money if they see this thing to the very end."

Alice sighed. "This is crazy! What we really ought to do is turn around and go home, Grandpa."

"I know," he said, "but I don't want to. I'd never forgive myself if I did that now. How about you?"

"I feel the same way."

"Good!" Jessie said. "Then it's settled. In a few more days we'll leave and drive the herd to San Miguel."

Buck shook his head. "Miss Starbuck, I never saw the likes of a woman like you. You just aren't about to quit for anything, are you?"

"No," Jessie said. "Like you and Alice, I lost a fine, loyal crew. That's why I won't stop until this cattle rustling and slave trading ring is destroyed completely—right down to the last man."

"And the last man," Ki added, "is Luke Lafitte."

★

Chapter 14

A few days later Jessie gathered the surviving gunfighters from Brownsville and told them of her plan to take the herd down to San Miguel.

"That's the craziest damn thing I ever heard of," one of the men protested. "I want no part of it. I just want to get paid off."

"Very well," Jessie said, and she paid the man. "Who else wants to be paid off, or who else would like to go on to San Miguel?"

There was a moment of indecision, and finally Tom said, "How much extra if we go on to San Miguel with the herd?"

"Another two hundred and fifty dollars," Jessie said.

"You won't live to pay us."

"Well, perhaps not, but with or without you, we're going. It's your decision."

Tom scowled and scratched his scarred cheek. "I've seen it this far, might as well see it the rest of the way."

"Good," Jessie said. "Are there any others?"

Only three of the other gunmen from Brownsville volunteered, and Jessie tried to hide her disappointment. She paid the others off, including those that were wounded, and then she, Ki, and the rest of them gathered up the small herd and drove them south, deeper into Mexico, toward San Miguel.

The weather turned very hot and humid. The longhorns moved along well and the little herd made good time.

"How much farther?" Jessie asked their captive outlaw at the end of five days.

"Just another couple miles."

"All right," Jessie said. "We're going to drive the herd in as if we stole them and intend to deliver and sell them to Lafitte."

Allen raised his wrists, which were bound with rawhide. "Gonna look a little funny if I'm tied up like this. They know me, ma'am. If they see my wrists bound together, they'll know that something fishy is going on."

"All right," Jessie said. She motioned to Ki, who cut the bonds. "But if you attempt to warn the buccaneers you'll be the first to die."

Allen nodded. "I know that."

"Good. Just as long as you understand it," Jessie said. "Let's go."

They were all tense as they approached the town of San Miguel. Jessie and the others kept the herd tightly together, and as they drew nearer, they saw huge cattle pens.

"Does it matter which ones we use?" Jessie asked.

"Nope," Doug Allen said. "The way it's done is that whoever rustles a herd just brings it down and drives it into a pen. Buyers will be along directly."

"Good," Jessie said. She signaled, indicating which pen she wanted the herd driven into.

Their approach and arrival attracted no attention whatsoever, telling Jessie that rustled cattle herds brought down from Texas were commonplace.

126

When the cattle were all penned and watered and Jessie had bought some grain from freighters who had immediately shown up, she was ready for whatever would happen next.

She sidled over to Allen, who was being watched closely by the samurai. "All right, what now?"

"Patience. Soon a buyer will come," the outlaw explained. "Maybe a couple of 'em."

Jessie nodded. Allen looked at her closely. "They aren't going to like dealing with a woman. Maybe it'd be better if I dealt with 'em."

"No," Jessie said quickly. "I don't trust you that much."

Allen chuckled. "Actually you got no reason to, lady."

"Watch him closely, Ki," Jessie said as she moved aimlessly about, waiting for the first buyers.

She did not have long to wait. Within an hour, two men approached her with big smiles.

"Understand you're the one that owns these cattle, miss."

Jessie did not fail to notice the bold way their eyes raked her body. "They're my cattle, all right," she said evasively.

"How much you want?"

Jessie shrugged. She should have asked Allen what the typical price of cattle was, but now she would just bluff her way along.

"Five dollars a head."

"That's ridiculous!" one of the buyers exclaimed in a voice that sounded genuinely shocked.

The other buyer, hooking his thumbs into his suspenders, said, "Maybe you don't understand things down here. This is Mexico and we don't pay a hell of a lot for beef. Hides are worth more than the meat, and it don't matter that your cattle are fat or not."

Jessie looked the man right in the eye. "That's not what I heard. I heard you load them on ships and send them

127

down to Central and South America. I heard you make a big profit."

The man blinked, cleared his throat self-importantly, and said, "We make a little money. That's what it's all about, ain't it, lady?"

"Yes," Jessie said. "That is what it's all about and I intend to make a little money myself. Getting this herd didn't come easy. Some pretty good men died on the north side of the Rio Grande River."

"What the hell's a woman like you doing in this kind of business?"

"That's neither here nor there," Jessie said. "What I want to know is are you going to pay five dollars a head?"

"Hell, no. I'll pay three."

"Four," Jessie said.

"Nope."

"All right," Jessie said, "three. I've got five hundred head here, give or take a couple."

"We'll count 'em," the man said. He looked to his partner. "Count 'em up and tell me what you read."

A few minutes later the man came back. "It's five hundred and eight," he said.

The buyer wet the tip of his pencil, pulled out a little pad, and rapidly did some figures. "Comes to about fifteen hundred dollars," he said after a moment.

"It comes to fifteen hundred and twenty-four dollars," Jessie corrected, "and I want every penny."

The man whistled softly. "You're a tough woman to bargain with."

"Bullshit," Jessie said. "I imagine most people get five dollars."

"Four fifty," the man said with a wink as he counted out the money. "A first-time seller like you has got to expect to get skinned."

Jessie took the money and deposited it in her jeans. "Well," she said, looking around at Buck, Ki, Alice, and the rest, "I guess maybe we oughta just go into town and have ourselves something to eat and drink."

One of the buyers frowned. "Miss," he said, "this is a pretty rough town and you and that other gal are good-lookin' women. If I was you I'd just take my money and make fast tracks on back across the Rio Grande."

"We won't do that," Jessie said. "We came a long way; it's been a hard drive. We intend to have a good feed. Some of the men are a mite thirsty, too."

"You can say that again," Tom growled.

"Suit yourself," one of the buyers said with an indifferent shrug of his shoulders. "I just thought I'd warn you that there is no law here in San Miguel, and everyone is on their own."

"That's about what we figured," Jessie said.

She gathered up her men, and they mounted their horses and rode on into San Miguel, leaving the buyers with the cattle.

"You did that pretty well," Allen said softly. "Now are you going to let me go?"

"Nope," Jessie said. "You'd make a beeline straight to Luke Lafitte's folks and tell them why we're here in the first place."

"Lafitte's gone," Allen said. "His ships aren't resting in the harbor."

Jessie had been afraid of this answer. "All right," she said, "where is his hacienda?"

Allen turned and pointed to the south. "See that big hacienda down there on the point?"

"Yes."

"That's Lafitte's place."

Jessie, Ki, and the rest of them studied it closely. "All

129

right," she said. "After dark that's where we're going to go."

Allen shook his head. "You're just bound and determined to get yourself killed, aren't you?"

Jessie said nothing. Her attention was diverted by a sight that turned her stomach. She saw six women chained to a long pole that was suspended between the shoulders of two black men. The sorry congregation was moving steadily down the street, and no one was paying the slightest bit of attention. The slave women's eyes were cast toward the ground.

"What is that?" Jessie asked.

"Slaves," the man said. "Mexican slaves. Maybe some of them are Apache. I don't know—just slaves."

"Slaves," Jessie said, repeating the word, studying the women. "And they'll be taken south along with the cattle?"

"Yeah, and sold just like the cattle."

Jessie's voice hardened. "Doesn't it make you feel rotten to be a part of this?"

"There'd be slaves captured up in Mexico and in the Apache country and then brought down here and sold, whether or not I was a part of it," Allen said defensively. "I don't get the money for slaves. I never dealt with slaves. I just helped Coburn rustle cattle."

"He murdered people or else took them as slaves! Don't lie to me, damn you!"

Allen looked away, his facial expression bleak. It was all Jessie could do to ride her horse past the slaves without jumping down and trying to free them, and she knew that Ki, Alice, and Buck Williams felt the same way as she did. But, of course, they could do nothing except ride on and pretend not to notice or care.

When they were past the group, Allen said, "Over there

130

is a cantina that serves decent food."

"I've lost my appetite," Jessie said as they dismounted and tied their horses at the rail.

She looked back up the street, but the slaves and their captors had vanished.

"Will those women be put on one of Lafitte's ships?"

"Probably," Allen said, unable to meet her accusing eyes.

"Then there are even more incentives for us to stop the buccaneers from this awful trade."

Ki nodded, and so did Alice and Buck.

When they entered the cantina, they found it almost deserted. That was just fine as far as Jessie was concerned. They took a large table in the back where it was dim and cool, and then Jessie handed over to Buck the money she had received for the herd.

"This belongs to you and Alice," she said, "and I promise you I'll make up the difference after we return to Texas."

"Don't worry about it," Buck said. "I've seen enough to know that this is where we ought to be and that Lafitte is a man that needs killing."

"I know," Jessie sighed. "Just seeing those enslaved women who will probably never see their families again makes me realize how inhuman some men become. It's time we put an end to this on the Gulf Coast."

Everyone nodded, and when food arrived, they ate in silence. Jessie was not a bit hungry, but she chewed her food thoroughly and got as much down as she could.

"We'll wait until after dark," she said, "and then we'll pretend to ride out. When we get beyond sight of the town, we'll hook around and come in behind Lafitte's hacienda."

"You think we can take it without gunfire?" Buck asked.

"I know we can," Ki interrupted. "I don't care how many sentries there are. By tomorrow morning we'll be in control and not a soul in this town will know it."

Alice nodded and so did her grandfather. Jessie said nothing, for she certainly did not need to be convinced. She had seen the samurai in action.

They spent a few hours drinking beer and tequila in the cantina and talking softly about this thing and that.

They had no idea when Lafitte would return, and even less idea of what would happen after he did. True, the odds seemed stacked against them, and yet they had gotten John Coburn using the element of surprise. Jessie was quite sure that if everything went well and the samurai were able to overpower the guards and gain an entry without arousing gunfire, they really would be in a position to surprise the buccaneer when he returned to his lair.

After it grew dark, Jessie nodded to her companions, and they left the cantina, each silent and somber, lost in the wondering of what tonight would bring and if they would see tomorrow's dawn.

★

Chapter 15

They tied their horses in an arroyo where they could not be seen, and then Ki motioned everyone to gather around him.

"I will go in alone," he said.

But Tom objected. "You're going to need help. I'll go with you. As long as I'm in this thing, I want to see it is done right."

"I don't need your help," Ki said. "I prefer to do it—"

"I don't give a damn what you prefer!" Tom growled. "If you fail, my life is on the line too. I'm going with you, samurai."

Ki started to raise his hand, but Jessie shook her head. "No, let him go."

The samurai accepted her decision and led Tom off into the night. Ki moved slowly toward the adobe walls, which appeared to be about seven feet tall. He had not yet seen a guard, but he was sure there were several posted, quite probably at the corners. Ki felt quite sure that Lafitte's guards would not be very alert, given the unlikelihood of an attack. From all that Ki could determine, Luke Lafitte had ruled this pirate village of San Miguel for years without any serious rivals.

"Stay close," Ki whispered.

Tom growled a surly reply, but he did stay close, and when they reached the walls, Ki moved along silently, looking for some crack or fissure that might assist him in climbing over the top. Finding none, he crouched down beside the wall with Tom.

"All right," he whispered. "I want you to cup your hands and hoist me over the top."

"Well, how the hell am I supposed to get in then?" Tom demanded.

"I'll throw you a rope. Just stay down low and as soon as I find one, I'll toss it over for you."

"The hell with that! Why don't you open the front gate and let me in?"

"No," Ki said. "That would be ridiculous. Whoever was inside would be alerted."

Tom wasn't pleased, but since it was obvious that he was far too big a man for Ki to heave up over the top of the adobe wall, there seemed to be little choice.

"All right," he said, lacing his fingers together and coming to his feet. He stooped over and Ki placed his foot in Tom's hand.

"All right," Ki said, "now!"

The burly man heaved with all his might, and Ki was propelled straight up into the air. Ki could have easily flown right over the top of the adobe wall, but he grabbed the upper edge and clung to it for a moment. Then he slipped down. He fell silently into the inner courtyard. There was still no sign of a sentry.

Ki crouched. He reached inside his tunic for a *shuriken* star blade, then began to move toward the corner of the

134

compound, sure that that was where he would find his first sentry, because it was the spot nearest the gate.

The samurai's reasoning was correct. In a few minutes he saw, sleeping on a parapet, a Mexican sentry with his gun propped up against the wall. Ki was pleased that he would not have to kill the man.

He reached for the sentry, fingers seeking the point on the upper part of the man's shoulder. Ki squeezed, and his fingers cut off the flow of blood to the sentry's brain. It was called *atemi,* and it was a very old and effective method of putting your opponent into a deep sleep. With the blood suddenly shut off from the brain, it went into a sort of coma.

Ki held the man's shoulder for a good long while, and he actually could have killed the man had he continued to apply pressure. But he stopped when he was satisfied that this sentry would pose him no problems for the rest of the night. Then he glided silently along the parapet, hunting for other sentries.

It did not take him long to find two more. They were smoking cigarettes and talking. Ki was disappointed, knowing he had no choice but to kill or at least severely disable both men.

He flattened down on the parapet and began to edge forward. From his limited Spanish, he realized the two men were making ribald jokes about the women they had seduced. The sentries were animated and still laughing when Ki leaped up and slammed the edge of his hand like an axe down upon the first man's neck. The neck made a small crunching sound, and the sentry died laughing.

Before his partner could even open his mouth to scream, Ki's foot arced forward in a sweep lotus that caught the second man in the throat. There was a strangling sound. The sentry grabbed his throat, and Ki delivered a short, hard punch that caught him squarely between the eyes and knocked him unconscious. Ki caught the man and eased him down beside his companion. He mashed out a burning cigarette, then continued on around the parapet, intent on circling the entire compound.

It all took Ki less than ten minutes, and when he was satisfied that there were no more sentries, he dropped down to the courtyard, then sprinted to the front gate, which he unbarred.

Tom was waiting. "How many?" the big man asked.

"Three," Ki said.

"And you killed them all?"

Ki ignored the question. "Come on, there are more inside sleeping."

Tom drew his six-gun. "We'll take care of them in a hell of a hurry."

"No," Ki said, grabbing the man's muscular arm. "We have to do this in silence, remember? Otherwise we'll wake up everyone in San Miguel and lose our element of surprise."

"Yeah, okay, dammit," Tom grumbled, holstering his six-gun. "Lead off!"

Ki led the way into the house. The front door was standing open, and as he crept along the dim hallways, every fiber of his body was alert.

They arrived at what Ki supposed was a bedroom. The samurai pushed the door open and peered inside. There was enough moonlight that he could see a couple sleeping together on the bed. Ki put his fingers to his lips, moved slowly over to the two of them, and then used *atemi* on both.

"What the hell did you do?" Tom asked in a hard whisper.

"I put them to sleep."

"How?"

"Never mind," the samurai said, moving out of the room and closing the door behind him. "Come along, let's find the rest."

If the samurai had had his way, he would have used *atemi* on every single member of the household. Unfortunately, however, in one bedroom a man was stirring about, and when they entered, he let out a shout and jumped for his six-gun. Before Ki could move, Tom's knife came up and the big man lunged forward, the knife slicing upward toward his belly. There was a low, anguished scream as Tom gutted the man, then hurled him aside.

"You put them to sleep for a while," he bragged to the samurai. "I put them asleep permanently."

Ki turned away in disgust. It went against his grain to kill men needlessly. In the faint moonlight, he'd seen a bloodlust in Tom that made him very uneasy.

Within twenty minutes they had overpowered all the rest of the household, and thanks to Ki, no one else had died. Instead, they were all carried to one room, then bound, gagged, and locked inside where they could not sound an alarm.

"All right," Ki said, "I think everything is in order now. We might as well go get Jessie and the others."

Tom nodded and they left the hacienda. But then, to their great surprise and distress, a buccaneer suddenly emerged from the livery.

"Hey, there! What the—"

Instinctively Tom drew his gun and Ki whirled, having seen it come up and knowing the foolish outlaw would pull the trigger. The samurai's hand slashed downward and Tom grunted in pain. The impact of Ki's hand on his wrist caused Tom's finger to jerk reflexively, and his gun emptied a bullet into the dirt.

137

The startled buccaneer spun around and raced toward the gate, screeching like a scalded cat. Ki forgot about Tom and his hand and reached into his tunic. With a flick of his wrist, a star blade was sent spinning through the moonlight. It caught the fleeing buccaneer in the back of the neck. He took two faltering steps and then crashed headfirst into the gate.

Tom was furious. "Damn you! I wasn't gonna shoot him. I was just going to pull my gun so he didn't run!"

"Well, how was I supposed to know that?" Ki demanded. "Now the whole town has probably been alerted."

"Aw, hell," Tom growled. "There's guns fired every night when these Mexicans get likkered up. They ain't gonna give one gunshot a second thought."

Ki could only grind his teeth in anger and hope that Tom was right. There was no doubt that the shot had been heard in San Miguel, but also no doubt that gunfire was commonplace both here at the hacienda and in the town itself.

"Let's go," Ki said, moving toward the gate.

As they passed the dead man, Ki plucked his *shuriken* star blade from the back of his neck, and there was anger in his voice when he spoke. "This really shouldn't have happened."

"You sure can throw that son of a bitch," Tom muttered. "I never seen anything like it. What do you call it?"

"It's called a *shuriken* star blade," Ki said, so disgusted that he really did not even want to talk to the cold-blooded man from Brownsville.

Tom must have sensed Ki's anger, because he clammed up. They left the hacienda and hurried toward where Jessie and the others were waiting.

"We heard a shot," Jessie said as soon as they were joined. "What happened?"

"It was an accident," Ki said when Tom offered no explanation. "For some reason, a buccaneer was in the livery. He saw us first and took off running and shouting toward the gate. It couldn't be helped, Jessie."

Even in the moonlight Ki could see the relief on Tom's face. The man was brutish, he was cruel, and there was bloodlust in him, but he did have some pride, and he knew he'd made a crucial mistake when he'd fired his gun.

"Hopefully," Jessie said, "no one heard the shot or, if they did, thought nothing of it. Let's go."

Ki and Tom remounted their horses, and they all rode into the hacienda, barring the gate behind them. The first thing they saw was the dead buccaneer, and Alice averted her eyes as they rode around the body and boarded the horses in the livery.

Ki immediately took Jessie to the room where the hostages had been bound and gagged. They were all still unconscious.

"Nice work," Jessie said to both the samurai and Tom.

"So what do we do now?" Tom asked.

"We wait," Jessie replied. "We just keep Lafitte's people under close guard and we wait."

It was clear by the look on Tom's scarred face that he didn't like waiting. "Maybe there's at least some liquor and we can use some of them women." Tom was thinking of the two servant women that Ki had rendered unconscious.

"No," Jessie said harshly. "You'll leave those women alone!"

Tom licked his lips. "You're too free with your orders, ma'am. But maybe I won't take me one of those Mex women. I *will* have some liquor if it's here to be found. How about it, boys?"

The other Brownsville gunmen nodded with challenging eyes. "We deserve a little party after this," one said.

"Damn right," said another.

When the men left, Jessie said, "We're going to have to keep a close eye on all three of those men—especially Tom."

"Sam and Dave will follow his lead," Ki said. "They'll do whatever Tom says because they're afraid of him. We can't trust any of them."

"I know that," Jessie said. "Let's just hope that Lafitte returns very soon."

Ki surveyed the unconscious hostages. "I'm sure that some of these people will know when Lafitte is expected back."

"Maybe," Jessie said. "As for right now, we might as well get some sleep. Who knows? We might even awaken to find Lafitte sailing into the harbor."

"That would be nice," the samurai said. "The sooner we get this over, the better."

Jessie agreed because she wanted to settle this matter one way or the other. "Good night," she said, patting Ki's arm and heading off to find a bedroom, "and nice work. I know that you did the hardest part."

The samurai said nothing. "I'm sorry about the gunshot."

"It wasn't your fault," she said. "I knew it was Tom's mistake the minute I saw your faces."

Ki was inwardly pleased to know that Jessie had such faith in him. He headed for the parapet where he would stand guard for the rest of the night. In the morning, when the others awakened, Ki would find a quiet place to catch a few hours' sleep, but until then, he would keep a watchful eye out on the peaceful harbor of San Miguel.

140

★

Chapter 16

The next few days passed uneventfully, although the atmosphere inside the buccaneers' fortress was very tense. It was clear to Jessie that if the hostages ever managed to escape, they would go on a killing rampage until Jessie and her friends were all put to death. Therefore, they could not relax for a moment.

At the end of three days, Jessie was finally rewarded when she saw the billowing white sails of a pair of pirate ships approaching from the south.

"Could it be them?" she asked hopefully.

"I think so," Ki said. "Let me go get Allen."

Allen was brought up to the parapet immediately to study the ships.

"Well?" Jessie demanded.

"That's Lafitte all right."

"Are you sure?"

"Of course I'm sure," Allen snapped.

"So what will he do now?" Jessie asked, feeling her heart begin to race. The ships looked so formidable she couldn't help but wonder if she and her handful of supporters stood any chance at all of defeating such a large, savage force as these fierce buccaneers.

"They'll sail into the harbor and drop anchor. Then, they'll lower boats and leave just a few men on board before they come up here. They'll be expecting the gates to be swung open in welcome."

"Oh, we'll welcome them all right," Jessie said, looking at the samurai and then at Alice and then at Buck Williams.

"Damn right we will," Tom grumbled off to one side. "I'll personally welcome Lafitte with a bullet."

"Now hold on," Jessie said quickly. "We're not going to just open fire on Lafitte and his buccaneers the moment they step inside. This won't become a turkey shoot."

But Tom disagreed and was ready to argue. "Listen, Miss Starbuck, they're going to outnumber us, maybe three, four to one, ain't that right, Allen?"

Allen nodded quietly.

"See, he knows that! So we gotta shoot 'em down once they get inside. Otherwise, they'll have time to draw their weapons and we'll all be cut down and quartered. These buccaneers are *fighting* men, ma'am! They'll never surrender to our puny few."

"We *must* give them a chance to throw down their weapons," Jessie stubbornly insisted.

"Dammit!" Tom said angrily. "You're gonna get us all killed if we don't gun them down when they walk through those gates! It's our only chance!"

"He's right," one of the other gunfighters said nervously. "We got lucky with John Coburn and his gang. But this time, there's just too many for us to handle."

Jessie's fists clenched at her side as she surveyed the last of the Texas gunfighters she'd hired. "Men, you've been a big help and you've come a long way, but if you don't want

142

to take my orders, I'll pay all of you off right now and we'll be done with each other. With a little luck, the buccaneers will never catch you and you'll reach Brownsville alive."

Tom almost did quit. Everyone could see that he wanted to, but something stopped him. "No," he finally said. "I'll stay, but if there's any sign at all that they're gonna fight, I say we gotta shoot first and ask questions later."

Jessie looked at the other men. "Are you men still with me?"

"How much you paying us if we stay?"

"A thousand dollars," Jessie said without hesitation. "A thousand dollars to each of you if we come out of this alive."

The gunfighters exchanged glances. Tom nodded his head. "I'm in. What about you, Dave?"

"Yeah."

"Me too," said the third man. "But I don't think much of our chances."

"Maybe they're better than we think," Tom said with a smile. "Maybe we can improve 'em just a little."

"What does that mean?" Jessie demanded.

"Never mind," Tom said, walking away as the other two gunfighters followed.

When Tom walked away, Jessie looked at the samurai. "I'm worried about him. I'm afraid that he's just going to open fire the minute Lafitte and his men are inside the gate."

"I'll stay close to him," Ki said.

Jessie looked at Allen. "I think you'd better go back inside. Ki, why don't you go with him?"

Allen blushed with anger. "Haven't I proven that I can be trusted yet?"

"No," Jessie said bluntly, "you have not. Take him away, Ki."

With Ki and Allen gone, just Alice and her grandfather were left. All three of them watched closely as the ships loomed larger and sailed gracefully into the harbor. Jessie saw the anchors thrown overboard, and just as Allen had said, a few minutes later longboats were lowered.

"They're not going to waste any time," Jessie said. "I think we had better make our preparations."

"But what can we do?" Alice asked.

"We can get Tom and the others up on the parapets. We can make sure that the hostages we've taken are all securely bound and gagged. We can't afford to make any mistakes that would alert the buccaneers. We *must* get the drop on them."

An air of excitement and danger quickly pervaded the hacienda. Jessie's men hurried to fill her orders. All the hostages were taken care of and a guard was posted over them. Everyone else took to the parapets, checking their weapons one last time.

By the time they were ready, Jessie could count eight longboats that were being rowed from the ships to the dock at San Miguel. When the longboats landed, she immediately recognized Luke Lafitte from Allen's description. He was tall, slender, and wore a red waistcoat. Lafitte was hatless and she saw that he had black hair. He was, even at this distance, a rather handsome man.

The infamous buccaneer hiked gracefully up the beach as his men fell in at his side. True to what Jessie had been told, Lafitte was wearing a long, curved saber. She could hear laughter and see that Lafitte was smiling. He looked almost youthful and happy, but she wondered how anyone could look that way after having sold slaves.

"All right," she called out softly, "stay down low. Ki, open the gate a little."

The samurai dashed down to ground level. He unbarred

the gate, opened it, then rushed up to the parapet. There, he had his samurai bow and quiver full of arrows.

The arrows in Ki's quiver were of many shapes and sizes, and the arrowheads were unlike anything that had ever been seen before on the North American continent. One was called "chewer," and its head was shaped like a corkscrew. It was designed to be fired at the midsection of an enemy, so that it could chew his bowels to pieces.

There was another Ki called "cleaver." Instead of coming to a point, this arrowhead was a crescent-shaped wafer of steel designed for severing ropes, or harness, or anything that would bind either horses or men together. In Japan, Ki explained, the cleaver was often used to cut down an enemy's battle flag and so completely demoralize his forces.

Perhaps the most frightening of all the arrowheads was "death's song." Death's song was so named because it had a small ceramic bulb fitted just behind the arrowhead. The bulb had little holes in it that caught the wind in flight, so that death's song whistled eerily until the moment when it struck its intended victim. To Jessie the sound of death's song was something akin to a cross between the world's largest mosquito and a violin string being tortured. Its pitch was so shrill it made dogs howl, and it also had a devastating psychological effect on the enemy.

Ki could fire the arrows at an unbelievably rapid rate, in the *inagashi* style, one of the highest skills learned by the samurai.

Jessie looked at her other men and saw that they all had pistols and Winchesters. Perhaps some of them were thinking that the samurai was out of his mind to be using a bow and arrow, when rifles and guns were available. They were, of course, absolutely wrong. In the hands of the samurai the bow and his terrible arrows would wreak more damage and create more panic among the buccaneers than all their firearms combined.

"Here they come," Jessie said, raising her head just slightly above the stockade wall and hearing the voices of the buccaneers and pirates as they swaggered boisterously up the hill toward the fortressed hacienda.

"Hello the hacienda!" Lafitte called in English, though his voice was accented heavily with Spanish. "Hello the hacienda!"

When there was no answer, Jessie had a desperate craving to raise her head and see what the buccaneer's reaction might be, but she knew to do this would be foolish. So she kept her head down, as did her men, and waited.

Again a call. "Hello the hacienda! Pablo? Why isn't this gate open wide in greeting?"

There was a small degree of concern in Lafitte's voice now, and when there was no reply, Jessie knew that he'd be weighing heavily what might be waiting inside. And yet, she could hear their boots as Lafitte and his men kept moving forward. Jessie supposed that Lafitte had been here so long, and had been so unchallenged by any enemies, that it never quite occurred to him that his own hacienda could be used to trap him.

So, to her great relief, Jessie watched as the buccaneers came marching on in, shouting and yelling for their servants.

Jessie's gun was tight in her fist, and she was about to call out for Lafitte and his men to raise their hands and freeze, when suddenly the scar-faced Tom bellowed, "Goddam you, Lafitte. I'll have your hide!" And with that he opened fire from the parapet.

Jessie shouted, but the sound of her voice was lost in the explosion of gunfire. She saw Lafitte spin, grab his arm,

146

and then hurl himself through a window. The yard below was chaos as the buccaneers realized they had walked into a trap. Tom and two other Brownsville gunfighters rained a deadly volley of bullets down on the men, using one extra pistol after the other, so they wouldn't have to reload. It was like shooting fish in a barrel, and the screaming buccaneers died in droves, many of them with the samurai's arrows in their chests. The blue gunsmoke was so thick and the frenzied cries so loud that everything was in total confusion for several moments. It was exactly the kind of slaughter that Jessie had hoped to avoid. But once set in motion, there was no stopping it until the last buccaneer was dead.

Jessie felt Ki grab her arm, and then they were racing down the stairway and across the yard, dodging bullets and dying men.

"What about Alice?" she cried. "What about Buck?"

"They're all right," the samurai yelled, pushing Jessie inside a building and then tearing an arrow from his quiver. Jessie heard death's song's familiar whine as it sailed across the courtyard to drive deep into a buccaneer's heart.

When the hammer of her Colt fell on an empty cylinder, Jessie knelt, reloaded, and began to fire again. The smoke was so thick that she could not tell how many of the buccaneers were down, but she did not see how very many men could still be alive, given the slaughter she'd first witnessed from the parapets.

"Wait here," Ki yelled, suddenly jumping forward as he fired another arrow.

Jessie's mind raced. Where had the samurai gone? Where were Alice and her grandfather? What about Tom? Had that fool died in the first volley?

There was no way of answering any of these questions until this desperate battle was either won or lost. Jessie watched a shadow flit across the yard. She almost fired,

147

until she realized it was Ki, and right behind him came Alice and her grandfather. They were halfway across the yard when Alice stumbled. The samurai stopped, doubled back, grabbed Alice by the arm, and literally carried her along. Her grandfather was trying to help, but suddenly he cried out and threw up his arms, then crumpled in death.

"No!" Alice screamed, her voice echoing clearly across the yard. She tried to stop and tear away from the samurai, but Ki propelled her forward, throwing her through the doorway. Alice bounced off the far wall and collapsed to the dirt, sobbing.

Ki slammed the door behind him and jumped over beside Jessie. "Things are not going well," he said. "I'm afraid that we're about all that there is left and there are still a few buccaneers standing."

"What about Tom?"

"I saw him lying facedown in the courtyard."

"None of this should have happened," Jessie swore.

"That may be true," Ki replied, "but it hardly matters anymore."

Jessie knew the samurai was right. All that mattered now was their survival. Having been attacked, Jessie knew that the buccaneers would show them no mercy. This was a fight to the death.

"We've got to get out of here," Ki said. "Our only chance left is to bargain our lives for those of the hostages."

Jessie helped Alice to her feet. "Your grandfather wouldn't want you to die! Hurry! You must come with us now!"

Alice was dazed but still seemed to understand. She hurried up with Jessie and the samurai as they charged into the hacienda. They moved quickly toward the hostages, but just before they reached that door, two buccaneers jumped into the hallway and Jessie fired instinctively. One screamed and the other disappeared. Then Jessie, Ki, and Alice burst into the room where they'd kept the hostages.

"What the hell's going on out there?" cried the lone gunman whom Jessie had left to guard them. "Are we all being slaughtered? What—"

"Settle down," Jessie said, slamming the door behind her. "We're not finished yet."

"Finished yet!" the gunfighter shrieked. "What's gone wrong!"

"Quiet!" the samurai said. He looked around at the hostages, one of which was Doug Allen. Ki pulled him to his feet and undid his gag. "All right," he said, "you're going to help us escape with our lives."

"The hell I will," Allen said.

At that moment, the Brownsville gunfighter bolted from the room and ran to save his life.

"Let the fool go," Jessie said.

Ki reached back and slapped Allen so hard that he broke the cattle rustler's lips. Allen glared at him, blood running down his chin.

"You're finished," he said with malicious satisfaction. "I'd be insane to help you."

Ki reached for his *tanto* blade, and Jessie was sure the samurai would slit the man's throat, but she held her tongue. Ki put the blade hard enough against Allen's gullet to cause bleeding and said, "You'll either help us or I'll cut you from ear to ear right now. Which will it be?"

Allen broke out in a cold sweat. His eyes bugged, and he seemed to have difficulty breathing as he looked into the samurai's dark, angry eyes.

"All right," he whispered, "I'll help."

"How do we get out of here?"

"Down the hall to the right there's a secret passage. It's always been here."

149

"That's what I thought," Ki said. "A pirate would have a secret passage. Let's go!"

When they shoved the door open, the hall was empty. Jessie, Ki, and Alice, with their hostage, started down the hallway. They passed quickly back out through the kitchen and into a large study.

"There!" Allen cried. "That bookcase pulls back."

Ki grabbed and pulled.

"No," Allen shouted. "Grab on the other side."

Ki did as he was told. The bookcase moved slightly.

"Harder!"

"Help him," Jessie commanded.

Allen jumped forward. "My goddam hands are tied, remember?"

Ki slashed the bonds that secured Allen's wrists, and together the two men pulled the bookcase away from the wall to reveal a large opening.

"Where does this lead?" Jessie asked.

"It leads under the adobe walls and comes out about fifty yards to the north of us in a stand of cottonwood."

"Let's go!" Jessie ordered, again sensing hope.

They hurried into the secret passage. Ki and Allen pushed the bookcase shut behind, plunging the escape tunnel into absolute darkness. Suddenly, Jessie heard racing footsteps and knew Allen had broken away in the darkness and was fleeing for his life. He alone knew the passageway; he alone would be able to run full tilt.

"Get after him, Ki!" Jessie shouted, grabbing Alice and moving forward as quickly as she dared, hands outstretched, feeling.

Jessie heard the samurai begin to run, and then suddenly she heard the sound she had dreaded—the sound of Ki's body striking a rock wall. She heard the samurai moan, and a few minutes later, when they reached him, she saw that he was crumpled on the ground, obviously dazed.

"Allen's escaping," Ki mumbled. "I'm sorry I couldn't . . ."

"Never mind," Jessie said, kneeling in the darkness, her hands moving over the samurai. "Can you move?"

"I'm all right," Ki said, struggling to his feet.

Jessie put her arm around him, and together the three of them made their way down the passageway until they saw a round circle of light.

"There it is!" Jessie shouted.

The beckoning light gave them hope, and they began to move faster. The light grew stronger, and when they finally reached the exit, it seemed blinding. They climbed up a small wooden stairway and found themselves hidden by a grove of trees about a quarter mile from San Miguel.

Jessie looked around, but there was no sign of Doug Allen. She knew the man had probably raced back to the hacienda and even now was seeking out Lafitte.

"We haven't much time," Jessie said. "They'll be coming for us very quickly."

"What are we going to do?" Alice whispered, trying to maintain her badly shaken composure.

"We're going to fight," Jessie said.

There was a moment of silence, and the samurai, who was cradling his bloodied head, looked up and said in a weak tone of voice, "Leave me."

"Never!" Jessie cried.

"Leave me," the samurai said. "Draw them away from here, and if you must be captured, let it happen. When I can regain my senses, I'll come to your rescue."

Jessie abhorred the idea of leaving Ki behind, but she could see that the samurai was helpless. He had apparently run fully upright into the tunnel wall. It was painfully obvious to Jessie that she had no choice but to make a

151

run for it with Alice and try and draw the buccaneers away from the helpless samurai.

"Come on!" she said, grabbing Alice's hand. "Let's run for town."

But even as she said this and they both began to run, Jessie knew there was no hope of escape and that, very soon, they would belong to the buccaneers.

★

Chapter 17

Jessie and Alice ran all the way into San Miguel, but even before they reached the town itself, they were spotted from the fortress by the buccaneers.

"In here!" Jessie called, jumping into an abandoned shack on the edge of the Mexican village. "Reload!"

Alice was breathing so hard she could barely straighten, so when Jessie finished reloading her own weapon, she took Alice's Colt and made sure that it was reloaded as well.

"Let's go!" Jessie ordered.

"Where?"

"To hide, if we can," Jessie replied. But when she swung the door open, she could see that the buccaneers were already racing to intercept her. Jessie slammed the door shut. "We've got only two choices. We can surrender or die."

"Maybe," Alice whispered, "death would be preferable to falling into the hands of those monsters."

"It would," Jessie said, "except for the samurai. If we surrender, it will divert attention from Ki. That way, he might be able to avoid detection until he can recover. And as long as he is free, we have a chance."

Alice nodded. "I say we do as Ki asked and surrender."

"I agree," Jessie said. "Let's just hope that they don't . . ."

"Yes," Alice managed to choke.

Jessie took a deep breath and opened the door. With her gun still clenched in her fist, she stepped outside to face the onrushing buccaneers. There were about ten of them, and they were more fearsome in appearance than John Coburn's rustlers had ever imagined themselves to be. Most of the buccaneers wore rings in their ears and noses, and some were horribly scarred from the sword and knife fights they'd waged.

"That's far enough," Jessie warned, raising her gun and pointing it at the front runner.

The buccaneers skidded to a halt, and the largest of them, a tall, bald fellow who was missing both ears, shouted, "Throw down that gun, woman, and tell us who ye be or we'll make you wish you were dead!"

"We demand to see Luke Lafitte," Jessie said, trying to sound as if she were unafraid.

The buccaneers fanned out in front of her and Alice. They bristled with weapons of all kinds, swords and old percussion pistols, dirks and long Spanish knives.

Their bald leader licked his lips like a dog about to chew a bone. "Woman, take off your clothes before I do it with me knife!"

Jessie cocked back the hammer of her six-gun. "Try it and I'll shoot your balls off, Baldy."

The buccaneers liked that and burst into coarse laughter. The bald one colored and took a menacing step forward, leaving Jessie no choice but to aim at his crotch and pull the trigger.

Her bullet tore a big hole at the apex of the buccaneer's

154

trousers. Blood exploded from his mangled organs, and the buccaneer screamed in agony and collapsed to writhe on the ground, hands cupping what had been his intact manhood. The other buccaneers, depraved sorts accustomed to the rawest kind of savagery, nonetheless drew back in shock.

Jessie again cocked the hammer of her six-gun. She had this motley crew's respect and she did not mean to lose it. "Who will take us to see Luke Lafitte?"

"We'll take you," a man said, "but not as long as ye be armed."

"I'll give up my arms only to Lafitte," Jessie said. "And the same goes for my friend."

The buccaneers, after a quick conference, agreed. Keeping a wide berth of Alice and Jessie, they escorted them back up to Lafitte's fortress, leaving their bald friend to bleed to death in the dirt.

Lafitte was waiting. His black eyes flashed when he saw Jessie, and he stood with his legs apart, watching her with a mixture of respect, lust, and anger.

"We took no prisoners here," Lafitte said. "Maybe you women can tell us who you are and who is behind this bloody trap."

Jessie had no intention of telling her real name. If Lafitte knew her real identity, Jessie was sure the buccaneer would ask a king's ransom for her safe return to Texas.

Jessie raised her chin. Her green eyes flashed with anger. "My name is Mrs. Appleworth," she blurted, knowing it sounded false.

"Mrs. Appleworth?" Lafitte asked, his lips forming a twisted grin of derision.

"That's right," Jessie repeated. "Mrs. Appleworth. And this is my sister, Alice."

"Come, come," Lafitte said, moving forward, a hand on the hilt of his sword. "Do you know who I am?"

155

"Yes. You are a descendant of Jean Lafitte, the famous buccaneer, and I suppose you think you are also famous, but you are not. You're just a common murderer. A dealer in slaves."

Lafitte's face clouded with anger. "You have a sharp tongue, madam."

He turned to Alice, reached out, lifted her chin, and looked into her eyes. "My, my! You are also lovely! Mr. Allen," Lafitte called.

A moment later Doug Allen appeared with a smirk on his lips. "Did you hear that?" Lafitte asked.

"I did, sir."

"Then who are these people?"

Doug Allen marched forward and leered at Jessie. "This is Jessica Starbuck, owner of the famed Circle Star Ranch in Texas. And this other woman—well, she's a nothing. She and her grandfather had this herd of cattle that we brought down. You must have seen them in the pens when you marched up from the town."

"Yes," Lafitte said, "I did."

"That was their herd," Allen said.

"But no more," Lafitte chuckled. "Well. So I get a herd of cattle and I get two beautiful women. This must be my lucky day."

"Lucky day!" Jessie stormed. "How many men did you lose?"

"Far more than you," Lafitte conceded, "but considering we walked into a trap, I think we did quite well, don't you?"

Jessie said nothing. Lafitte reached out and encircled her small waist with his arm. "I think, my dear, that if you cooperate nicely, your life may be spared."

"I'll never cooperate with you," she spat, pulling away from the roguish buccaneer.

156

"In that case," Lafitte said, "I think we're going to have to hand you over to my men. A night or two with them will kill your spirit."

Jessie's blood chilled. She heard cruel laughter all around her and understood what her horrible fate would be if the buccaneer leader allowed his men to have their way with her body.

"So," Lafitte said, noting the stricken look on Jessie's face, "perhaps you're having second thoughts."

Jessie said nothing. Lafitte stepped up close again. He leaned forward, and his lips brushed her cheek and then moved to her neck, as he whispered in her ear, "I think, my dear, that you would find me much more satisfactory than all this common rabble."

Jessie stiffened. It was all she could do to keep from lashing out at this man.

Lafitte stepped back a little. "Come, ladies," he said, "I will show you to my room."

They followed the buccaneer because there was no choice. When they entered Lafitte's bedroom, he closed the door behind them and then leaned up against it, a smile on his lips.

"I will enjoy you both at the same time," he said, his eyes visually raping them.

Alice shrank back in fear, but Jessie stood her ground. "You'll have to kill us first."

"My dear," Lafitte answered, "that would be a terrible waste. I think you'll change your mind, given a few days. You'll find me charming and generous. There are thousands of women who beg to be allowed to lie in my bed for just an hour."

"Well, I'm not one of them," Jessie said, "and neither is Alice."

"That will change," Lafitte said confidently, "and I wish

that I could do something about it right now, but unfortunately I have much to do. My ship is in the harbor awaiting my instructions. There are the cattle to be loaded, slaves and other matters to attend to, not to mention the dead that must be buried. But don't worry," Lafitte added, as he started to leave, "I will make sure that your dead are buried also."

"Thank you," Jessie snapped.

"You're welcome." Lafitte bowed slightly at the door, his hand again on the hilt of his sword, and then with a small chuckle he turned and left. As he passed out of sight, Jessie heard him order two men to stand guard, both inside and outside, by the window. She and Alice were to be guarded both day and night.

When the door closed behind Lafitte, Alice threw herself into Jessie's arms and they held each other tightly.

"Will he be back tonight?" Alice asked.

"I don't know," Jessie said, but she imagined he would.

"What can we do?"

"We need to think," Jessie said, "and we need to be calm."

She led Alice over to Lafitte's bed, and they sat down side by side. "We must keep our wits," Jessie said. "We are alive," and then lowering her voice, she added, "and the samurai is alive as well."

"What can he possibly do? Despite killing so many, there are still more than a dozen."

Jessie tried to comfort the young woman. "With the samurai," she said, choosing her words carefully, "the odds never have mattered. Ki will find a way to reach us as soon as he is able."

"But will he be able?" Alice asked. "He looked so terrible. His face—"

"He was dazed and battered," Jessie said, cutting the young woman off. "Yes, there was blood on his face, but the samurai, as you know, has extraordinary powers of recovery. Mark my words, Alice, he will come to our rescue."

"Are you sure?"

Jessie gazed out through the window. Already the two new guards were posted. "Yes," she said, thinking about how those two men would be the first to die. "The samurai will be here soon after dark and then we will be free again."

Alice found the courage to nod. "I believe in you," she said, "and I believe in Ki."

"Good," Jessie said quietly. "Now let us be still and rest, for there is much ahead before this night is through."

Chapter 18

The samurai found water and washed his face. He cleared his senses late that afternoon and then he rested. When darkness came, he slipped up the hill, back through the groves, and then moved to the secret passage that he, Jessie, and Alice had emerged from seven hours before, when they had fled the hacienda. Ki was not surprised to discover that there were no guards at the secret entrance. After all, they had pulled the bookcase back in place and there was no reason to suspect that Lafitte, in all the excitement, would expect anyone to return through the passageway.

The samurai descended the stairs into the passageway, moving slowly and deliberately, hands outstretched. It was still pitch-black, yet he had come this way before and now knew the twists and turns of the tunnel.

When he finally reached the far stairs, he knew he was under the hacienda and that only the bookcase separated him from entering the hacienda itself. He put his shoulder to the bookcase and was able to lever it from the wall, farther and farther, until at last he slipped into the room.

Where would Lafitte be keeping Jessie and Alice hostage? The answer came to Ki almost immediately. In the man's bedroom, of course. And the real question was would Lafitte be in there with them? Ki hoped not. He could not imagine Jessie submitting to such a man, and yet to save her life and Alice's, Ki knew that Jessie would submit to almost anything.

He moved out of the study and down the hallway. Two men appeared, and Ki ducked back into a bedroom and flattened himself against the wall until they passed. As he approached Lafitte's bedroom, he saw two sentries in the hallway. There was no way of catching them by surprise. The hallway was too narrow and it was illuminated by candles.

Ki returned to the other bedroom, then exited by the window. He circled around the hacienda but again found two guards, waiting outside Lafitte's bedroom window. Now, however, the samurai had room to maneuver. Ki drew his *tanto* blade and crept slowly forward. He could hear the two guards talking, and then suddenly he launched himself, knife flashing. There could be no error. No chance that his blade would miss, or not render the guards completely silent. His blade did its deadly work, and the guards were both dead before they fell.

Ki jumped through the window into Lafitte's bedroom so fast that he was able to clamp his hand over Alice's mouth before she cried out with surprise and alarm.

"It's all right," he said, "we're getting out of here."

"Thank God you're here!" Jessie exclaimed. "Luke Lafitte is coming back. Now all we have to do is wait for him."

"Wait?" the samurai asked.

"Yes," Jessie said. "This isn't finished until he is dead or captured and returned to Texas for crimes against her people. He'll hang for certain."

The samurai wanted to protest, but he knew better.

161

Besides, Jessie was right. Lafitte had to be stopped once and for all.

And so they waited and waited, until almost midnight. Then suddenly they heard Lafitte's laughter as he talked to the hallway guards, probably making some ribald comment about the two Texan beauties inside who would soon enjoy his sexual appetite, whether they wished to or not.

Ki slipped behind the bed, and when the door was opened, Lafitte stepped through just as boldly and arrogantly as always. His eyes flashed and he grinned broadly.

"Well, my beauties, I was hoping that you would be waiting in my bed. But, since I see you are not, perhaps it is just as well. I enjoy undressing my women."

Jessie said nothing. Her heart was beating fast as the buccaneer entered the room. With a flourish he unbuckled the saber at his side, laid it ceremoniously across a bureau, and then advanced on Jessie.

"Shut the door," he called back over his shoulder to his guards. "This beauty is for my eyes alone tonight. Perhaps tomorrow night you can have your pleasure."

The guards giggled obscenely and shut the door.

Lafitte came to Jessie's side. "Now, my beauty," he said, "let's see your body first."

Jessie froze. She tried to keep her breathing normal, but it was almost impossible. She allowed Lafitte to touch her face, then her neck, and then her bosom. The pirate's fingers began to unbutton her blouse and peel it away. Jessie waited until Lafitte's eyes were a little glazed with desire, then she said, "Anytime now, my dear."

Ki, hiding behind the bed, knew exactly what Jessie meant. With a lunge he threw himself over the bed, and his hands went directly for the buccaneer's throat. Caught off-guard and without his saber, Lafitte staggered. He tried to hack at the samurai, but he found that Ki's fingers

162

were already digging into his throat. The buccaneer was very strong. He landed on his back with Ki on top. They rolled, Ki desperately trying to keep the man from shouting a warning to his guards.

Lafitte's hand groped for a knife and tore it loose. He slashed awkwardly at the samurai, and Ki smothered a cry of his own, as he felt his flesh being rent. And then the samurai released his grip for just an instant and slammed his hand down on the man's windpipe in a crushing blow.

Lafitte's eyes bugged. He slashed again at the samurai's ribs. Ki pounded the man once more in the throat, this time with his doubled fist. Lafitte's mouth flew open and he sucked for air that would not come. The samurai, not wanting to see the buccaneer suffer, reached under Lafitte's neck with one hand and grabbed his hair with the other. With a quick twist, he snapped the buccaneer's neck.

Jessie and Alice both heard the sickening pop. The samurai stood up.

"You've been cut!" Alice exclaimed.

"I'm all right," Ki assured her. "We must get out of here!"

Alice and Jessie did not need urging, and they followed Ki in retracing his steps out Lafitte's window, into another bedroom window, and back to the study. The bookcase was still protruding slightly from the wall, and they squeezed through the opening; then all three of them struggled to pull it shut. But before they did, Jessie saw a kerosene lamp and spilled its entire contents across the floor, then put a match to it. The study burst into flames, consuming the room in a hot flash.

"This hacienda will burn to the ground before the buccaneers can put out the flames," she said. "It will never be anyone's stronghold again!"

Ki agreed, and they hurried back into the passageway, feeling the heat of the inferno on their backs. Once in the trees again, they saw flames licking the sky over the fortress walls.

"With Lafitte and most of his buccaneers dead, San Miguel is finished," Ki remarked.

"If it isn't," Jessie replied, "I'll bring my crew down here and we'll wipe the rest of them out forever."

Jessie turned to Alice. "We'll get horses and then recover your herd."

"What!" Alice asked with surprise.

"You heard me," Jessie said. "I'm not about to leave your cattle behind now."

"All right," Alice said quickly.

The samurai nodded. "It's going to make things a little more difficult."

"We'll manage," Jessie said.

When they reached the edge of San Miguel, they found a livery, and while Ki rendered its owner unconscious through the use of *atemi,* Jessie and Alice caught and saddled three horses. Minutes later they rode out to the cattle holding pens. Silently, they opened the gates and drove Alice's herd out.

"It's a good thing they're already trail broke," Jessie said. "We'll drive them back north to Brownsville."

And that was exactly what they did. They got the cattle moving north in the moonlight, every once in a while glancing over their shoulders at the huge flames now consuming the fortress walls.

Every now and then the samurai would ride back a mile or two to check their backtrail and make sure they weren't being followed. By dawn they saw the outskirts of Matamoros.

"What'll we do now?" Ki asked. "There are bound to be outlaws in Matamoros, and when they see this herd, they're going to want to take it back."

Jessie thought about how if they tried to skirt the town, they would be seen and outlaws of every description would attempt to stop them from crossing the Rio Grande back into Texas with Alice's herd of fat cattle.

"All right," Jessie said, "why don't we stampede these cattle right through them?"

"Through Matamoros?" Alice asked, in shock and surprise.

"Exactly," Jessie said.

Ki exchanged glances with Alice, and both nodded, slow grins forming on their weary faces.

The samurai said, "This will long be remembered in Matamoros."

"It sure will," Jessie said. "Let's go!"

And with the town of Matamoros less than a half a mile ahead, Jessie drew her gun and fired twice into the sky. The samurai whooped, and Alice also emptied shots into the air.

The Texas longhorns bolted ahead in fear. They ran straight up the road leading into town, and when they struck the edge of the Mexican border town, they entered it as if through a huge funnel. They jammed the main street, bawling and stomping, knocking over wagons and anything in their way. Mexicans and gringos alike shouted curses at the three Americans as they drove the cattle on through town. A few shots were fired harmlessly in Jessie's general direction, but the dust was so thick Jessie had no fear they'd be shot.

In only a few minutes, they were blowing out of town and leaping into the warm, shallow Rio Grande River. "Head 'em off to the south towards the wharf south of Brownsville!" she called.

And the herd swept around the town and onto the beach. The citizens in Brownsville, awakened by the shouts and gunfire coming from Matamoros, surged out of their homes and hotels. Jessie paid them no mind, because nothing would stop them now. She was back in the United States, and somehow she would find another small herd to buy and add to this one. Within a week, with any luck at all, she would have a thousand cattle on boats headed for New Orleans. Better late than never, she told herself as the cattle raced on. And better alive than dead!

Watch for

LONE STAR AND THE AZTEC TREASURE

123rd novel in the exciting LONE STAR series
from Jove

Coming in November!

SPECIAL PREVIEW!

Giles Tippette, America's new star of the classic Western, tells
the epic story of Justa Williams and his family's struggle for
survival . . .

Gunpoint

By the acclaimed author of *Sixkiller, Hard Rock,* and *Jail-
break.*

*Here is a special excerpt from this riveting new novel—
available from Jove books . . .*

I was standing in front of my house, yawning, when the messenger from the telegraph office rode up. It was a fine, early summer day and I knew the boy, Joshua, from a thousand other telegrams he'd delivered from Blessing, the nearest town to our ranch some seven miles away.

Only this time he didn't hand me a telegram but a handwritten note on cheap foolscap paper. I opened it. It said, in block letters:

I WILL KILL YOU ON SIGHT JUSTA WILLIAMS

Joshua was about to ride away on his mule. I stopped him. I said, "Who gave you this?" gesturing with the note.

He said, "Jus' a white gennelman's thar in town. Give me a dollar to brang it out to you."

"What did he look like?"

He kind of rolled his eyes. "I never taken no notice, Mistuh Justa. I jest done what the dollar tol' me to do."

"Was he old, was he young? Was he tall? Fat?"

171

"Suh, I never taken no notice. I's down at the train depot an' he come up an ast me could I git a message to you. I said, 'Shorely.' An' then he give me the dollar 'n I got on my mule an' lit out. Did I do wrong?"

"No," I said slowly. I gave his mule a slap on the rump. "You get on back to town and don't say nothing about this. You understand? Not to anybody."

"Yes, suh," he said. And then he was gone, loping away on the good saddle mule he had.

I walked slowly back into my house, looking at the message and thinking. The house was empty. My bride, Nora, and our eight-month-old son had gone to Houston with the balance of her family for a reunion. I couldn't go because I was Justa Williams and I was the boss of the Half-Moon ranch, a spread of some thirty thousand deeded acres and some two hundred thousand other acres of government grazing land. I was going on for thirty years old and I'd been running the ranch since I was about eighteen when my father, Howard, had gone down through the death of my mother and a bullet through the lungs. I had two brothers: Ben, who was as wild as a March hare, and Norris, the middle brother, who'd read too many books.

For myself I was tired as hell and needed, badly, to get away from it all, even if it was just to go on a two-week drunk. We were a big organization. What with the ranch and other property and investments our outfit was worth something like two million dollars. And as near as I could figure, I'd been carrying all that load for all those years without much of a break of any kind except for a week's honeymoon with Nora. In short I was tired and I was given out and I was wishing for a relief from all the damn responsibility. If it hadn't been work, it had been a fight or trouble of some kind. Back East, in that year of 1895, the world was starting to get sort of civilized. But along the

172

coastal bend of Texas, in Matagorda County, a man could still get messages from some nameless person threatening to kill him on sight.

I went on into the house and sat down. It was cool in there, a relief from the July heat. It was a long, low, Mexican ranch-style house with red tile on the roof, a fairly big house with thick walls that Nora had mostly designed. The house I'd grown up in, the big house, the house we called ranch headquarters, was about a half a mile away. Both of my brothers still lived there with our dad and a few cooks and maids of all work. But I was tired of work, tired of all of it, tired of listening to folks whining and complaining and expecting me to make it all right. Whatever it was.

And now this message had come. Well, it wasn't any surprise. I'd been threatened before so they weren't getting a man who'd come late in life to being a cherry. I was so damned tired that for a while I just sat there with the message in my hand without much curiosity as to who had sent it.

Lord, the place was quiet. Without Nora's presence and that of my eight-month-old heir, who was general screaming his head off, the place seemed like it had gone vacant.

For a long time I just sat there, staring at the brief message. I had enemies a-plenty but, for the life of me, I couldn't think of any who would send me such a note. Most of them would have come busting through the front door with a shotgun or a pair of revolvers. No, it had to be the work of a gun hired by someone who'd thought I'd done him dirt. And he had to be someone who figured to cause me a good deal of worry in addition to whatever else he had planned for me. It was noontime, but I didn't feel much like eating even though Nora had left Juanita, our cook and maid and maybe the fattest cook and maid in the county, to look after me. She came in and asked me in Spanish what I wanted to eat. I told her nothing and, since she looked so disappointed, I told her she could peel me an apple and fetch it to me. Then I got up and went in my office, where my whiskey was, and poured myself out a good, stiff drink. Most folks would have said it was too hot for hard liquor, but I was not of that mind. Besides, I was mighty glum. Nora hadn't been gone quite a week out of the month's visit she had planned, and already I was mooning around the house and cussing myself for ever giving her permission to go in the first place. That week had given me some idea of how she'd felt when I'd been called away on ranch business of some kind or another and been gone for a considerable time. I'd always thought her complaints had just come from an overwrought female, but I reckoned it had even been lonelier for her. At least now I had my work and was out and about the ranch, while she'd mostly been stuck in the house without a female neighbor nearer than five miles to visit and gossip with.

Of course I could have gone and stayed in the big house, returned to my old ways just as if I were still single. But I was reluctant to do that. For one thing it would have meant eating Buttercup's cooking, which was a chore any sane man would have avoided. But it was considerably more than that; I'd moved out and I had a home and I figured that was the place for me to be. Nora's presence was still there; I could feel it. I could even imagine I could smell the last lingering wisps from her perfume.

Besides that, I figured one or both of my brothers would have some crack to make about not being able to stand my own company or was I homesick for Mommy to come back. We knew each other like we knew our own guns and nothing was off limits as far as the joshing went.

But I did want to confer with them about the threatening note. That was family as well as ranch business. There was nobody, neither of my brothers, even with Dad's advice, who was capable of running the ranch, which was the cornerstone of our business. If something were to happen to me we would be in a pretty pickle. Many years before I'd started an upgrading program in our cattle by bringing in Shorthorn cattle from the Midwest, Herefords, whiteface purebreds, to breed to our all-bone, horse-killing, half-crazy-half-wild herd of Longhorns. It had worked so successfully that we now had a purebred herd of our own of Herefords, some five hundred of them, as well as a herd of some five thousand crossbreds that could be handled and worked without wearing out three horses before the noon meal. Which had been the case when I'd inherited herds of pure Longhorns when Howard had turned the ranch over to me.

But there was an art in that crossbreeding and I was the only one who really understood it. You just didn't throw a purebred Hereford bull in with a bunch of crossbred cows and let him do the deciding. No, you had to keep herd books and watch your bloodlines and breed for a certain conformation that would give you the most beef per pound of cow. As a result, our breeding program had produced cattle that we easily sold to the Northern markets for nearly twice what my stubborn neighbors were getting for their cattle.

I figured to go over to the big house and show the note to my brothers and Howard and see what they thought, but I didn't figure to go until after supper. It been our custom, even after my marriage, for all of us to gather in the big room that was about half office and half sitting room and sit around discussing the day's events and having a few after-supper drinks. It was also then when, if anybody had any proposals, they could present them to me for my approval. Norris ran the business end of our affairs, but he couldn't make a deal over a thousand dollars without my say-so. Of course that was generally just a formality since his was the better judgment in such matters. But there had to be just one boss and that was me. As I say, a situation I was finding more and more wearisome.

I thought to go up to the house about seven of the evening. Juanita would have fixed my supper and they would have had theirs, and we'd all be relaxed and I could show them the note and get their opinion. Personally, I thought it was somebody's idea of a prank. If you are going to kill a man it ain't real good policy to warn him in advance.

About seven I set out walking toward the big house. It was just coming dusk and there was a nice breeze blowing in from the gulf. I kept three saddle horses in the little corral behind my house, but I could walk the half mile in just about the same time as it would take me to get up a horse and get him saddled and bridled. Besides, the evening was pleasant and I felt the need to stretch my legs.

I let myself into the house through the back door, passed the door to the dining room, and then turned left into the big office. Dad was sitting in his rocking chair near to the door of the little bedroom he occupied. Norris was working at some papers an his side of the big double desk we shared. Ben was in a straight-backed chair he had tilted back against the wall. The whiskey was on the table next to Ben. When I came in the room he said, "Well, well. If it ain't the deserted bridegroom. Taken to loping your mule yet?"

I made a motion as if to kick the chair out from under him and said, "Shut up, Ben. You'd be the one to know about that."

Howard said, "Any word from Nora yet, son?"

176

I shook my head. "Naw. I told her to go and enjoy herself and not worry about writing me." I poured myself out a drink and then went and sat in a big easy chair that was against the back wall. Norris looked up from his work and said, "Justa, how much higher are you going to let this cattle market go before you sell off some beef?"

"About a week," I said. "Maybe a little longer."

"Isn't that sort of taking a gamble? The bottom could fall out of this market any day."

"Norris, didn't anybody ever tell you that ranching was a gamble?"

"Yes," he said, "I believe you've mentioned that three or four hundred times. But the point is I could use the cash right now. There's a new issue of U.S. treasury bonds that are paying four percent. Those cattle we should be shipping right now are about to reach the point of diminishing returns."

Ben said, "Whatever in the hell that means."

I said, "I'll think it over." I ragged Norris a good deal and got him angry at every good opportunity, but I generally listened when he was talking about money.

After that Ben and I talked about getting some fresh blood in the horse herd. The hard work was done for the year but some of our mounts were getting on and we'd been crossbreeding within the herd too long. I told Ben I thought he ought to think about getting a few good Morgan studs and breeding them in with some of our younger quarter horse mares. For staying power there was nothing like a Morgan. And if you crossed that with the quick speed of a quarter horse you had something that would stay with you all day under just about any kind of conditions.

After that we talked about this and that, until I finally dragged the note out of my pocket. I said, not wanting to make it seem too important, "Got a little love letter this noon. Wondered what ya'll thought about it." I got out of

177

my chair and walked over and handed it to Ben. He read it and then brought all four legs of his chair to the floor with a thump and read it again. He looked aver at me. "What the hell! You figure this to be the genuine article?"

I shrugged and went back to my chair. "I don't know," I said. "I wanted to get ya'll's opinion."

Ben got up and handed the note to Norris. He read it and then raised his eyebrows. "How'd you get this?"

"That messenger boy from the telegraph office, Joshua, brought it out to me. Said some man had given him a dollar to bring it out."

"Did you ask him what the man looked like?"

I said drily, "Yes, Norris, I asked him what the man looked like but he said he didn't know. Said all he saw was the dollar."

Norris said, "Well, if it's somebody's idea of a joke it's a damn poor one." He reached back and handed the letter to Howard.

Dad was a little time in reading the note since Norris had to go and fetch his spectacles out of his bedroom. When he'd got them adjusted he read it over several times and then looked at me. "Son, I don't believe this is something you can laugh off. You and this ranch have made considerable enemies through the years. The kind of enemies who don't care if they were right or wrong and the kind of enemies who carry a grudge forever."

"Then why warn me?"

Norris said, "To get more satisfaction out of it. To scare you."

I looked at Dad. He shook his head. "If they know Justa well enough to want to kill him they'll also know he don't scare. No, there's another reason. They must know Justa ain't all that easy to kill. About like trying to corner a cat in a railroad roundhouse. But if you put a man on his guard and keep him on his guard, it's got to eventually take off some of the edge. Wear him down to where he ain't really himself. The same way you buck down a bronc. Let him do all the work against himself."

I said, "So you take it serious, Howard?"

"Yes, sir," he said. "I damn well do. This ain't no prank."

"What shall I do?"

Norris said, "Maybe we ought to run over in our minds the people you've had trouble with in the past who've lived to bear a grudge."

I said, "That's a lot of folks."

Ben said, "Well, there was that little war we had with that Preston family over control of the island."

Howard said, "Yes, but that was one ranch against another."

Norris said, "Yes, but they well knew that Justa was running matters. As does everyone who knows this ranch. So any grudge directed at the ranch is going to be directed right at Justa."

I said, with just a hint of bitterness, "Was that supposed to go with the job, Howard? You didn't explain that part to me."

Ben said, "What about the man in the buggy? He sounds like a likely suspect for such a turn."

Norris said, "But he was crippled."

Ben gave him a sour look. "He's from the border, Norris. You reckon he couldn't hire some gun help?"

Howard said, "Was that the hombre that tried to drive that herd of cattle with tick fever through our range? Those Mexican cattle that hadn't been quarantined?"

Norris said, "Yes, Dad. And Justa made that little man, whatever his name was, drive up here and pay damages."

Ben said, "And he swore right then and there that *he'd* make Justa pay damages."

I said, "For my money it's got something to do with that maniac up in Bandera County that kept me locked up in a root cellar for nearly a week and then tried to have me hung for a crime I didn't even know about."

"But you killed him. And damn near every gun hand he had."

I said, "Yeah, but there's always that daughter of his. And there was a son."

Ben gave me a slight smile. "I thought ya'll was close. I mean *real* close. You and the daughter."

I said, "What we done didn't have anything to do with anything. And I think she about as crazy as her father. And, Ben, if you ever mention that woman around Nora, I'm liable to send you one of those notes."

Norris said, "But that's been almost three years ago."

I shook my head. "Time ain't nothing to a woman. They got the patience of an Indian. She'd wait this long just figuring it'd take that much time to forget her."

Norris said skeptically, "That note doesn't look made by a women's hand."

I said, "It's block lettering, Norris. That doesn't tell you a damn thing. Besides, maybe she hired a gun hand who could write."

Ben said, "I never heard of one."

Howard said, waving the note, "Son, what are you going to do about this?"

I shrugged. "Well, Dad, I don't see where there's anything for me to do right now. I can't shoot a message and until somebody either gets in front of me or behind me or *somewheres,* I don't see what I can do except keep a sharp lookout."

The next day I was about two miles from ranch headquarters, riding my three-year-old bay gelding down the little wagon track that led to Blessing, when I heard the whine of a bullet passing just over my head, closely followed by the crack of a distant rifle. I never hesitated; I just fell off my horse to the side away from the sound of the rifle. I landed on all fours in the roadbed, and then crawled as quick as I could toward the sound and into the high grass. My horse had run off a little ways, surprised at my unusual dismount. He turned his head to look at me, wondering, I expected, what the hell was going on.

But I was too busy burrowing into that high grass as slow as I could so as not to cause it to ripple or sway or give away my position in any other way to worry about my horse. I took off my hat on account of its high crown, and then I eased my revolver out of its holster, cocking it as I did. I was carrying a .42/.40 Navy Colt, which is a .40-caliber cartridge chamber on a .42-caliber frame. The .42-caliber frame gave it a good weight in the hand with less barrel deviation, and the .40-caliber bullets it fired would stop any thing you hit in the right place. But it still wasn't any match for a rifle at long range, even with the six-inch barrel. My enemy, whoever he was, could just sit there patiently and fire at the slightest movement, and he had to eventually get me because I couldn't lay out there all day. It was only ten of the morning, but already the sun was way up and plenty hot. I could feel a little trickle of sweat running down my nose, but I daren't move to wipe it away for fear even that slight movement could be seen. And I couldn't chance raising my head enough to see for that too would expose my position. All I could do was lay there, staring down at the earth, and wait, knowing that, at any second, my bushwhacker could be making his way silently in my direction. He'd have to know, given the terrain, the general location of where I was hiding.

Of course he might have thought he'd hit me, especially from the way I'd just fallen off my horse. I took a cautious look to my left. My horse was still about ten yards away, cropping at the grass along the side of the road. Fortunately, the tied reins had fallen behind the saddle horn and were held there. If I wanted to make a run for it I wouldn't have to spend the time gathering up the reins. The bad part of that was that our horses were taught to ground-rein. When you got off, if you dropped the reins they'd stand there just as if they were tied to a stump. But this way my horse was free to wander off as the spirit might move him. Leaving me afoot whilst being stalked by a man with a rifle.

I tried to remember how close the bullet had sounded over my head and whether or not the assassin might have thought he'd hit me. He had to have been firing upward because there was no other concealment except the high grass. Then I got to thinking I hadn't seen a horse. Well, there were enough little depressions in the prairie that he could have hid a horse some ways back and then come forward on foot and concealed himself in the high grass when he saw me coming.

But how could he have known I was coming? Well, that one wasn't too hard to figure out. I usually went to town at least two or three times a week. If the man had been watching me at all he'd of known that. So then all he'd of had to do was come out every morning and just wait. Sooner or later he was bound to see me coming along, either going or returning.

But I kept thinking about that shot. I'd had my horse in a walk, just slouching along. And God knows, I made a big enough target. In that high grass he could easily have concealed himself close enough for an easy shot, especially if he was a gun hand. The more I thought about it the more I began to think the shooter had been aiming to miss me, to

182

scare me, to wear me down as Howard had said. If the note had come from somebody with an old grudge, they'd *want* me to know who was about to kill me or have me killed. And a bushwhacking rifle shot wasn't all that personal. Maybe the idea was to just keep worrying me until I got to twitching and where I was about a quarter of a second slow. That would be about all the edge a good gun hand would need.

I'd been laying there for what I judged to be a good half hour. Unfortunately I'd crawled in near an ant mound and there was a constant stream of the little insects passing by my hands. Sooner or later one of them was going to sting me. By now I was soaked in sweat and starting to get little cramps from laying so still. I know I couldn't stay there much longer. At any second my horse might take it into his head to go loping back to the barn. As it was he was steadily eating his way further and further from my position.

I made up my mind I was going to have to do something. I cautiously and slowly raised my head until I could just see over the grass. There wasn't anything to see except grass. There was no man, no movement, not even a head of cattle that the gunman might have secreted himself behind.

I took a deep breath and moved, jamming my hat on my head as I did and ramming my gun into its holster. I ran, keeping as low as I could, to my horse. He gave me a startled look, but he didn't spook. Ben trains our horses to expect nearly anything. If they are of a nervous nature we don't keep them.

I reached his left side, stuck my left boot in the stirrup, and swung my right leg just over the saddle. Then, hanging on to his side, I grabbed his right rein with my right hand and pulled his head around until he was pointing up the road. I was holding on to the saddle with my left hand. I kicked him in the ribs as best I could, and got him into a

183

trot and then into a lope going up the road toward town. I tell you, it was hell hanging on to his side. I'd been going a-horseback since I could walk, but I wasn't no trick rider and the position I was in made my horse run sort of sideways so that his gait was rough and awkward.

But I hung on him like that for what I judged to be a quarter of a mile and out of rifle shot. Only then did I pull myself up into the saddle and settle myself into a normal position to ride a horse. Almost immediately I pulled up and turned in the saddle to look back. Not a thing was stirring, just innocent grass waving slightly in the light breeze that had sprung up.

I shook my head, puzzled. Somebody was up to something, but I was damned if I could tell what. If they were trying to make me uneasy they were doing a good job of it. And the fact that I was married and had a wife and child to care for, and a hell of a lot more reason to live than when I was a single man, was a mighty big influence in my worry. It could be that the person behind the threats was aware of that and was taking advantage of it. If such was the case, it made me think more and more that it was the work of the daughter of the maniac in Bandera that had tried in several ways to end my life. It was the way a woman would think because she would know about such things. I couldn't visualize the man in the buggy understanding that a man with loved ones will cling harder to life for their sake than a man with nothing else to lose except his own hide.

From the Creators of Longarm!

Featuring the beautiful Jessica Starbuck
and her loyal half-American half-
Japanese martial arts sidekick Ki.

___LONE STAR AND THE DEADLY VIGILANTES   0-515-10709-3/$3.50
   #111
___LONE STAR AND THE GHOST DANCERS #112   0-515-10734-4/$3.50
___LONE STAR AND THE HELLBOUND   0-515-10754-9/$3.50
   PILGRIMS #113
___LONE STAR AND THE TRAIL TO ABILENE #114 0-515-10791-3/$3.50
___LONE STAR AND THE HORSE THIEVES #115   0-515-10809-X/$3.50
___LONE STAR AND THE DEEPWATER PIRATES   0-515-10833-2/$3.50
   #116
___LONE STAR AND THE BLACK BANDANA   0-515-10850-2/$3.50
   GANG #117
___LONE STAR IN THE TIMBERLANDS #118   0-515-10866-9/$3.50
___LONE STAR AND THE MEXICAN MUSKETS #119 0-515-10881-2/$3.50
___LONE STAR AND THE SANTA FE SHOWDOWN   0-515-10902-9/$3.99
   #120
___LONE STAR AND THE GUNRUNNERS #121   0-515-10930-4/$3.99
___LONE STAR AND THE BUCCANEERS #122   0-515-10956-8/$3.99
___LONE STAR AND THE AZTEC TREASURE #123   0-515-10981-9/$3.99
   (Nov. 1992)
___LONE STAR AND THE TRAIL OF MURDER #124 0-515-10998-3/$3.99
   (Dec. 1992)

For Visa, MasterCard and American Express orders ($15 minimum) call: 1-800-631-8571

Check book(s). Fill out coupon. Send to:
BERKLEY PUBLISHING GROUP
390 Murray Hill Pkwy., Dept. B
East Rutherford, NJ 07073

NAME_____

ADDRESS_____

CITY_____

STATE_____ZIP_____

PLEASE ALLOW 6 WEEKS FOR DELIVERY.
PRICES ARE SUBJECT TO CHANGE
WITHOUT NOTICE.

POSTAGE AND HANDLING:
$1.75 for one book, 75¢ for each ad-
ditional. Do not exceed $5.50.

BOOK TOTAL $_____

POSTAGE & HANDLING $_____

APPLICABLE SALES TAX $_____
(CA, NJ, NY, PA)

TOTAL AMOUNT DUE $_____

PAYABLE IN US FUNDS.
(No cash orders accepted.)

200e

If you enjoyed this book,
subscribe now and get...

TWO FREE

A $7.00 VALUE–

If you would like to read more of the very best, most exciting, adventurous, action-packed Westerns being published today, you'll want to subscribe to True Value's Western Home Subscription Service.

Each month the editors of True Value will select the 6 very best Westerns from America's leading publishers for special readers like you. You'll be able to preview these new titles as soon as they are published, *FREE* for ten days with no obligation!

TWO FREE BOOKS

When you subscribe, we'll send you your first month's shipment of the newest and best 6 Westerns for you to preview. With your first shipment, two of these books will be yours as our introductory gift to you absolutely *FREE* (a $7.00 value), regardless of what you decide to do. If

you like them, as much as we think you will, keep all six books but pay for just 4 at the low subscriber rate of just $2.75 each. If you decide to return them, keep 2 of the titles as our gift. No obligation.

Special Subscriber Savings

When you become a True Value subscriber you'll save money several ways. First, all regular monthly selections will be billed at the low subscriber price of just $2.75 each. That's at least a savings of $4.50 each month below the publishers price. Second, there is never any shipping, handling or other hidden charges—*Free home delivery*. What's more there is no minimum number of books you must buy, you may return any selection for full credit and you can cancel your subscription at any time. A TRUE VALUE!

A special offer for people who enjoy reading the best Westerns published today.

WESTERNS!

NO OBLIGATION

Mail the coupon below

To start your subscription and receive 2 FREE WESTERNS, fill out the coupon below and mail it today. We'll send your first shipment which includes 2 FREE BOOKS as soon as we receive it.

Mail To: **True Value Home Subscription Services, Inc. P.O. Box 5235**
120 Brighton Road, Clifton, New Jersey 07015-5235

YES! I want to start reviewing the very best Westerns being published today. Send me my first shipment of 6 Westerns for me to preview FREE for 10 days. If I decide to keep them, I'll pay for just 4 of the books at the low subscriber price of $2.75 each; a total $11.00 (a $21.00 value). Then each month I'll receive the 6 newest and best Westerns to preview Free for 10 days. If I'm not satisfied I may return them within 10 days and owe nothing. Otherwise I'll be billed at the special low subscriber rate of $2.75 each; a total of $16.50 (at least a $21.00 value) and save $4.50 off the publishers price. There are never any shipping, handling or other hidden charges. I understand I am under no obligation to purchase any number of books and I can cancel my subscription at any time, no questions asked. In any case the 2 FREE books are mine to keep.

Name _____

Street Address _____ Apt. No. _____

City _____ State _____ Zip Code _____

Telephone _____

Signature _____
(if under 18 parent or guardian must sign)

Terms and prices subject to change. Orders subject to acceptance by True Value Home Subscription Services, Inc.

10956